The Rumphulus

The
Rumphulus

Joseph G. Peterson

University of Iowa Press
Iowa City

University of Iowa Press, Iowa City 52242
Copyright © 2020 by Joseph G. Peterson
www.uipress.uiowa.edu
Printed in the United States of America
ISBN 978-1-60938-730-3 (pbk)
ISBN 978-1-60938-731-0 (ebk)

Cover design by Kathleen Lynch/Black Kat Design
Text design by Omega Clay

Printed on acid-free paper

Cataloging-in-Publication data is on file
with the Library of Congress.

The Rumphulus

Part 1
Rumphulus

After she came for me and found me in the forest preserves and picked me up to take me away from here a second time, I regretted almost immediately having to leave these woods that for twenty-seven months or so had been my happy home. Indeed I regretted that moment when she first set eyes on me and decided it was me and no one else, there was no one else either in these forest preserves or in the world for that matter who would do. When she saw me she decided that everyone else in the world—all available candidates—would officially be excluded from her attentions forever or at least for as long as I remained the center of those attentions, and while I remained the center of those attentions the world as it is effectively didn't exist for her except as a context to fit me into and it existed for me only as something like a dream or—like the sunlight from a prisoner's window—it beaconed, and I knew that when I had found the will to do so I would escape back into it. Eventually.

It's interesting and I realized this almost immediately and I'll tell it to you right now because I want to tell the truth as well as I know it, but the day I first saw her I realized suddenly that life is a journey—to be sure—and we all journey upon the footpath of life, but more than a journey it's a sort of shopping spree that takes place in a tourist town at the far end of our journey and the reason we shop in this tourist town at the end of the road is more than anything to mark our journey's end. We must reach the end of the journey for that is why we travel, that is why we are on a journey in the first place—to reach the end but we reach the end because we seek something and what we seek at the end of the journey is a trophy of sorts so we go on this shopping spree when

3

we reach the far terminus of our journey and we shop because we must collect something, a trophy of some sort or another or what is commonly known as a tchotchke. We must collect our trophy on our shopping spree at journey's end so that we can bring it home with us and place it on our mantel or in our closet or on the shelf in our garage next to the oil cans for instance, or in our attic or under the bed to be pulled out infrequently pulled out from time to time as a reminder of where we've been or where we went that time way back when when we journeyed out into the world but—more often than not—once we arrive home the trophy is effectively discarded, or if not discarded left alone in its place where we left it on the shelf in the garage next to the oil cans or in the attic or under the bed that is very much its sleeping place and in that sleeping place it goes on like all the other trophies we collected from other journeys to fulfill its true destiny, which is merely to sit there in its sleeping place collecting dust announcing to no one and to nothing that it came from a far-off place and was collected once by someone traveling on a journey.

I was therefore made uneasy when she came for me that day—and it was rather clear to me the moment she set eyes on me—and I realized with some uneasiness that she was on a shopping spree of sorts and was coming to collect me as one of her trophies. It was my plight I realized. I was once a human but now rebuked by the world my only value to the world it seems, if I had any value to it at all—I thought—would be no more than the value of a trophy whose true destiny more than signifying the end of the journey is merely to sit discarded in some corner collecting dust and signifying to nothing and no one whence it came. I remember her coming for me that day and I could see it in her eyes I could see it even though she sat in her blue Pontiac

4

with the rusting chrome bumper several hundred feet from where I sat—see it even there—in her eyes across such a distance. That acquisitive look that said: the journey's end had been reached for her and now it was time to go shopping. Her face had that appraising sensibility. I could tell immediately that she was sizing me up trying to make a determination of whether I was the precise thing she was looking for to mark the end of her journey or whether some other victim out here in the woods a victim who had been rebuked by the world just as I had been rebuked by the world might be an even more fitting trophy.

But while she sat there appraising me there was this moment where her face resolved itself—and it happened so quickly—from an appraising face to an acquisitive face and it was that moment the moment her face went from an appraising face to an acquisitive face when I realized that not only had she come to collect me but that my true destiny my authentic role in the world as it stood now was not so much to be a human who had needs and wants of my own but to become a trophy—really *her* trophy—whose sole purpose was to eventually sit unused collecting dust unused in some forgotten corner of her house while she resumed whatever activities had previously consumed her before she had gone on her journey. Like fixing her teeth.

I was to be her trophy at the end of the journey for her— that much I saw and I suppose she saw something in my face a resolution I suppose you might call it a resolve to be what she wanted me to be. A willingness to capitulate. If I shall be a trophy I thought to myself then I shall be a trophy I remember saying to myself not long after she had collected me. And since it didn't require too much effort to collect me to begin with and bring me home to her house which was a derelict home on the edge of the

5

forest preserves and since also she had been spying on me for
several months prior to coming to get me and since this spying
this observing my strengths (my ability to persist out here alone
in the forest preserves) and my weaknesses (my ability to persist
out here alone in the forest preserves) was indeed the journey
whose end she wanted to mark by claiming me she made it known
once she had seen me and I had seen her that no other person
would do and that indeed for all intents and purposes it was a
shopping spree in a tourist town and she desperately had to have
me as some sort of trophy signifying the end of her journey. She
needed to have me above all others to be sure her eyes seemed
to say when that acquisitive look emerged almost imperceptibly
on her face. I was the one she was to collect and bring home to
her place. No other person would do. I was the one and none
of the others who were equally marooned in these godforsaken
woods could do. For what did they have to do with her journey
which was a journey of several months of spying on me? They
were at best ancillary figures on a stage that starred me in my
role as someone trying to get by day to day in these godforsaken woods or they were as billboards on the road that we pass
by—hardly noticing them but feeling nevertheless their collective
impact on our journey down that road—or they were even such as
historical points of interest so to speak. Part of the world that she
had found me in and therefore I suppose of some though not of a
fateful and enduring interest to her.

   Like me they each and every one of them god help them
had also been rebuked (some violently some not so violently but
all inexplicably) by the world and like me they each and every
one of them were stranded for indeterminate lengths of time in
these forest preserves. They like me were each struggling to get

by. Living day to day in their makeshift hovels and we all had our makeshift hovels that we would live in as if hiding during the night or during inclement weather but which we escaped from as often as we could escape from as if the hovels themselves were part of the plague part of our offense. Escape from as if we were escaping the very physical blot of our offense to the world and what were our offenses? Indeed this became the question the overriding question that took hold of our brains and would not let loose. All of us were offending figures but how we offended—way back when we were a part of the world—was never quite known by us. Our rebuke from the world had often happened with such swiftness and finality that it seemed in retrospect unbelievably absurd—so much punishment for so little or unknown offense. And when we saw each other in the woods as happened from time to time we would say to one another what was your offense and more often than not our question would be greeted by a puzzled stare and the response would invariably be a variation of that's what I'd like to know or I have no idea really or it just happened, I was rebuked by the world. What for? I cannot say. After a while of being in the woods and especially as we drifted away in time from that moment in the past when we were rebuked by the world each and every one of us marooned in these forest preserves felt dumbfounded that it had been us—or me—selected from all the rest out there for surely there must be more worthy offenders out there than us but we had been the ones selected out and rebuked for reasons that were inexplicable and unknowable to us. And together occasionally as the circumstances dictated we one on one or in small groups would socialize with one another in the limestone park building and we came to know who was who in these woods and what was what but no one ever had any

clear answers as to why us. Why so absolutely and continuously
rebuked for really we each felt we had never done anything grave
at all never done anything so grave other than to be exactly who
we were destined to be neither more nor less. And occasionally
Mike—for instance—who had been a tax collector in his past life
and who we all thought was a true sage or this other guy Adam
who had been a chiropractor for several years before he'd been
rebuked and who was really quite ingenious in the ways of the
world in his own way but one or the other of them Mike or Adam
would point out in a suppressed rage for we were all filled with
rage out there in the woods that we could barely contain—but
don't you see they Mike or Adam would say with tremendous
sagacity. And another an incredibly gentle soul Paul who had
been a priest in his former life before he'd been caught with child
molestation and rebuked by the world would point out: we aren't
understood is our problem he would say. We are misunderstood
and I suppose you could say—he would say—we are all in our way
misfits. And then others would say speak for yourself priest what
the hell do you know about it? And the priest would grow very
quiet and somber still not accustomed to the disrespectful tone
we all used around him but Mike would chime in: leave the father
alone. He's obviously right. Why else would we be out here if not
because we're misfits and we're misfits for the sole reason that
we are so determined and I don't say this lightly, he would say: we
are so determined to be exactly who we want to be nothing more
nor less. And I or someone else in the crowd would invariably
point out that if you truly looked at it it wasn't really our fault—
really—for we were made to be this way meant to be ourselves.
We were meant to be exactly who we were so to be punished
for who we manifest ourselves to be (ourselves) is really to be

8

punished for something that's not our fault at all. And it was this—this quality of it not being our fault that we chose to act according to our natures in fact it was our nature to do so that made the whole situation of our being rebuked so maddeningly incomprehensible to us. I didn't choose to be this way and yet I'm rebuked for being this way. It was madness plain and simple and as a result each of us walked around exiled in this little patch of wilderness with a permanent look of bafflement on our faces not to mention the barely contained rage that would sometimes boil over and you knew when the rage boiled over in one or another of us for there would be a scream. So many screams out there in those forest preserves but the most fearsome screams came from one of us who was stranded out in the wilderness alone and rebuked by the world and the screams unless you heard them yourself you would never believe they were human screams: they were terrifying and inarticulate like the howl of a wolf yet the howl we would hear in the night would be something that was closer to the pain and anguish of being permanently and inex-plicably rebuked by the world than the cry of a wolf that was a signal in part to other wolves. And the howl of one or another of the men out here, isolated and alone, would resound through the forest preserves until the rage or anxiety as the case may be that the howl had incarnated had at least for the time being been at least partially abated.

* * * *

So in many ways I was no different than they than these other fallen who were stranded and alone in the woods with no clear sense of how to get out of here. We were all fallen brothers

9

of a sort rebuked by the world and only she—Meredith—but she of everyone else out there in the world was alone in showing any interest whatsoever in any of us. She was the only soul from the outside world who seemed to care who or what we were and of everyone stranded here she had for some reason unbeknownst to me picked me from all of them and for a long time she cared almost exclusively only for me. Even though later she showed a passing if not a growing interest in all the others.

It was random really that she should select me out over one of them but as she later pointed out to me in her own quiet way her voice so beautifully quiet and subdued: I had to start some- where. And then later I realized, but this was much much later when I was looking out her bedroom window that had a view of the forest preserves and looking through her window I saw—and it was with a gasp that I saw it—but deep into the woods you could see through her window barely visible through the thick and brambly brush the exact location of my encampment. And so I had been chosen, I deduced at that point, and spied upon by her for no other reason than the most obvious one of all: that I happened to be the most convenient of all the people locked up in these forest preserves for her to spy upon. I was most con- venient because there I was in front of her window as if I had been a lion or a hyena or some other such African creature that had unwittingly made his home in front of the conservationist's camp on the Serengeti Plain. Only she wasn't a conservationist but what I can only describe as—for there are no other words for it—a spy and I, I was certainly very much like a lion or a hyena for a latent wildness had emerged from within me while I was out there living alone all those many months in the wilderness. But she was a spy and this discovery that I was being spied upon from her bedroom window was the beginning of my sense that these woods though I had construed them as my friends were in point of fact the furthest thing from it or in the words of that sage yet shady character Mike who had been locked up in these woods for possibly a decade or more: these woods are your absolute enemy. To think otherwise is to deceive yourself. And I laughed when he told me this for nothing seemed further from the truth but later— much later—I would see that he was accurate in his saying this; he was accurate with absolute precision and it was funny—later— when I realized just how accurate his prediction came to be. These woods are not your friend he would say from time to time and I would laugh at him but later after it was too late to say how right he was after it was too late to say to his face: Mike you were prescient on the issue of the woods as you have been prescient on so many things and I apologize for laughing at you laughing at what I had no idea to be your prescience; later I would reflect on his prescience and think just how foolish I was to believe the woods were my friend I was foolish then about the friendliness of the woods as I was foolish about so many things so very many things.

Her spying on me then—it was clear—was another bizarrely irrational thing just one of the many bizarrely irrational things that have been done to me throughout my life like being rebuked by the world which was also irrational and my rebukement by the world was not only difficult for me to comprehend but the wound it had inflicted upon me was forever gaping and fresh and I should say appalling. I chose you she later told me without so much saying it as pointing out her window with her finger indicating my hovel deep in the thicket of branches and brambles because I had to start somewhere and your camp just happened to be in view of

11

my bedroom window. And indeed it occurred to me that this was something the world might have told me if it were ever to explain to me exactly why it had rebuked me: I—the world might have said if it could articulate why it had so thoroughly and punishingly rebuked me—had to start somewhere and you were right there standing in front of me so what else could I do but rebuke you. And really my rebukement hardly seemed less random than this: that I had been in the wrong place at the right time.

These others in the woods were insofar as they had been rebuked by the world hardly different than I. Yet we were all radically different from each other. Some were more attractive than me like Adam the chiropractor for instance, and others were more savvy like Pauly who had been a mechanic in his former life and who seemed to exist in these woods with the greatest of ease and nonchalance and there were alpha types out here who though incredibly dominating in these woods with their magnetic personalities—Adam for example—had somehow failed to make it in the outside world. Others were stronger and more courageous than I: a Mexican named José for instance whom everyone called Hunter because a) he had the visage of an incredibly fierce warrior b) when we had group hunts he was invariably the leader of the hunts and c) when we weren't hunting he nevertheless seemed infinitely better at acquiring all modern conveniences by scrounging around the dumpsters finding things that no one thought possible to find. There was Mike too who as I've said was sagacious beyond belief. He was so fucking relentlessly truthful and honest you couldn't help being in awe of him and you also knew that one day he would end up like the common skunk—struck down as if he were roadkill and left to decay like all the other animals stranded out here in the very spot where he had fallen. Of all these characters none were more curious than the priest who'd been rebuked by the world on account of child molestation. The priest was infinitely more devout and holy than I or for that matter holier than anyone else stranded out here in this wilderness. Though he was endlessly persecuted in these woods he was like a shining light and I often found myself desiring in some remote place of my heart to be exactly like him: to be holy and devout and at odds with evil and to be conscious to the micro-unit of how at odds with evil I was. Yet I felt doomed also whenever I was around the priest for his goodness inevitably made me aware of my badness and I remember getting terribly annoyed as everyone in the woods did with the priest and there were times even when inexplicably an urge overcame me to lash out and strangle the priest for being so good and devout. But those feelings would invariably pass and a sort of awe for the holiness of the priest would overcome me and there were days I swore to myself I would do anything the priest asked me to do—I would walk through fire lie on a bed of nails or leap off cliffs just say the word—but the thing is the priest never requested anything of me or of any of us and I suppose this too, this not being asked by the priest to listen to the better angels of our nature made me and all the others too—I suspect—hate him in ways and with a violence and malevolence that are not so easy in retrospect to explain.

So there were all these characters who in one way or another were infinitely more deserving of the attentions of Meredith than I. Nevertheless she chose me the least among them—over all the rest. I believe they were of interest to her how could they not be?— but they were of interest to her only as figures who surrounded me and I was the star on the stage that she

13

was observing. She was interested in them but she was never interested in them for who they were in themselves. She was only interested in them so long as they provided some sort of context for understanding me. That's why I say they were, to her, essentially ancillary figures at best: historical points of interest so to speak that gave charm and a certain reality to the world she found me in. She even . . . after she took me back with her to her home, but from time to time she would even ask me about one or another of them and she was most interested in Mike. And of all the people stuck in the woods none interested her more than Mike yet cumulatively her interest for everyone in the woods was negligible compared to her interest in me alone. You might say she was hardly interested not even barely curious of all the others combined and this included Mike whom she was interested in—as well—in comparison to me. And yet . . . and yet this is the thing: at the end of the day her interest in me as a living breathing being with desires and wishes of my own was, to say the least, inconsequential for what she really saw in me that day was my willingness to go so far with her. She saw very clearly my willingness to capitulate, which was a willingness to become at the drop of a hat what she most wanted me to become: her trophy.

However for reasons I don't completely understand and which I don't believe she herself even completely understands she decided to spy—let me say that again she decided to *spy* on me from her bedroom window! She spied on me for many months without my knowing it and I believe she spied without knowing herself why she spied on me nor do I think she realized that her spying on me constituted for her some sort of journey, though over time I think she began to construe her spying on me as a journey of sorts, so when her cover was broken, when

14

she saw me seeing her sitting there in her blue Pontiac with the rusted chrome bumpers and dented hub caps, when she saw that I saw that she was spying on me for reasons that she herself probably couldn't explain—couldn't explain even if she had half a mind to—her journey as a covert spy was effectively over and the moment her journey ended she realized, for it must be some sort of instinct with travelers to shop, but she realized that she had to go on a spending spree so to speak and collect me in that so-called tourist town she found me in, which was essentially a little field and at the edge of that field there was a bench near the river. That day out in the forest preserves with her in her blue Pontiac car and me sitting ravaged by my bewilderment at being rebuked and a simmering rage that was amorphically directed toward the world sitting there on a picnic bench minding my own business I lifted my head and saw a blue Pontiac sedan come to a stop in a cul-de-sac at the dead end of the forest preserve road and without so much as thinking about what I saw I saw a woman who was not so absentmindedly gazing at me. When I saw her see me, when eye contact was made, from that moment forth my life was never the same again. Her cover was blown, her journey was ended and from that moment on my chief value to the world—if I had any value at all—was, I could see, to be nothing more than a trophy for her to collect bring home and then at some later point (and it happened sooner than I thought it might happen) I would, like all trophies, be forgotten and discarded somewhere somehow announcing to nothing and no one whence I came which was in fact the true destiny of all trophies collected at the far terminus point of a journey and I was a fool to know this and to simultaneously allow myself to be collected, but such was the state of my fallenness: I couldn't say no.

15

After she saw me see her she knew immediately that I would go with her. She could see more clearly than even I could see just how beaten down by the world I had been. I was utterly ruined, living alone out in these godforsaken woods. Ruined because I had been rebuked by the world. Never in my life had I ever been chosen for anything which was part of the reason I was out in these godforsaken forest preserves to begin with but that day because I had felt such terrible and unending resentment not to mention barely suppressed rage toward a world that had seemingly with universal accord rebuked me—and rebuked me for no reason that I have ever been able to surmise—and sent me out here in the wilderness to feast on locusts so to speak for a forty-day period of time that became many more than forty days and looked until that day I had seen her see me to be an interminable and indeterminate length of time—indeed I felt permanently stuck and trapped in these woods stuck so I didn't know how I would ever escape them, didn't know how until that moment I saw her seeing me and then I thought I saw a way out: she, I thought to myself—thought in a flash, thought so quickly it wasn't thought at all, but instinct. I instinctively saw that she, this woman Meredith, sitting there alone in her blue Pontiac car was my ticket out of here. She is the person I've been waiting all my life for I thought to myself with instinctive urgency. Waiting waiting with diminishing hopes of ever finding her and now when I least expected it when I had all but given up hope of ever finding her she arrives out of nowhere so to speak—she arrives to collect me. And I couldn't resist, really! I couldn't resist the invitation her eyes made to me that day when, while I was sitting on the park bench overlooking the river I saw her see me—caught her spying calculating my strengths my weaknesses and how best to broach this situation, which was

16

the situation of one—Meredith—coming perhaps out of her own desperation to collect me and bring me home with her as some sort of claim that she had been on this journey that consisted of several months of spying on me and now after several months of being on that journey of espionage she had reached her journey's end both metaphorically and literally for she had driven all the way to the dead end of the forest preserve road and sat with her blue Pontiac idling in the little cul-de-sac that formed the far terminus point of the forest preserve road looking out across the field to the bench where I sat near the river. She reached the end of her journey and the end of the forest preserve road simultaneously so naturally she must have some trophy or other to show for it and thus necessarily she came and collected me and as I say who was I—I who had been rebuked and all but forgotten by the world—but who was I on this earth in this godforsaken place but who was I to say no? And I'll tell you who I was I was exactly what the world told me I was. I was a nothing and I was a nobody and the world told me this so long so often that I came to believe it and this telling me of my nothingness and nobodiness was the exact form my rebukement from the world had taken. It's my being a nobody and a nothing in the world's view that landed me here in these forest preserves in the first place no way out. What's more while I lived in these forest preserves and as it became increasingly clear that I would never escape these woods I became increasingly convinced of my own servile worthlessness. And like all other servile and worthless souls I ask you this: who am I to believe I have any powers of autonomy my own powers of nay-saying? Who am I? And I'll tell you who I am: I'm an absolute nobody and like all other absolute nobodies I did what was most instinctive for me to do that day when she saw me, I did what

17

seemed right for me to do at the time: I followed the path of least resistance and when she said, come come on back home with me so I can collect you like a trophy and place you in a glass case, I merely capitulated and off, I mean easier than I thought possible—off—we went off driving in her blue Pontiac off driving through the woods.

* * * *

Oh sure there was the whole issue of the asking. The whole issue of her getting out of her car walking the several hundred feet across the park to stand next to me by my picnic bench that I sat upon. There was the whole issue of her breaking down my defenses by offering me a toke from her pot pipe and she knew as well as I knew that there was no saying no. I was spineless really even though I had real and genuine issues about going back home with her.

Here she says offering me the pot pipe after traversing the field that separated us. Here she says with that beautiful and gentle voice of hers so quiet and unobtrusive. Here, her voice gentle as a lamb's that voice comforting me out in the wilderness like nothing ever before or since has ever comforted me. And it was that more than anything the comforting sound of her voice and the comfort of her body as she stood near me inclined toward mine that I found so difficult to rebuff. Torching up her pot pipe and leaning in toward me while shielding herself from the wind, she took a toke and handed it to me strands of hair fluttering across her face. Here, she says pushing her hair away, I brought you this. Take a hit if you'd like and so I did because I liked and she sat down next to me and we sat there a while watching the river roll by and I'm a little high and so is she and I'm a little mixed up because her spying like this on me concerns me and in the back of my head is a little voice telling me that each moment I spend with her each word I exchange with her only makes me more inextricably hers because, and this is the point: who am I and I know I am nobody but who am I to say no to the alarming comfort of her presence her voice so calm and soothing, her body so close and I could see it in her eyes that this is more than mere comfort and soothingness that she's offering. I could see by looking into her eyes that look that was a look of incredible acquisitiveness of an unabating hunger to possess me.

A long silence and then she breaks it. So—she says with a sweeping gesture of her thin arm that seemed to encompass everything: the river sparkling before us the woods that disappear into darkness behind us (where my hovel is broken down and very carefully with incredible meticulousness hidden from view) and the sky and the ground—you live here. And as she spoke I paid special attention to those wispy sounds in her voice trying to figure out just exactly how she was going to locate herself in relation to me and for a moment a brief moment I thought I heard a quiet note of disapproval in her voice. I mean is it really true that a man a grown man can spend his days out here? And though she didn't say this I thought for a moment that she might say it, but in the end she just stayed quiet listening for something, perhaps for an answer or perhaps, like me, she wasn't paying attention to any particular thing at all but instead was absorbed by everything though in retrospect like me I think she was waiting for an answer and when it was clear none was forthcoming she merely said: I'm high. She turned her head slowly as though it were a slice of coconut cream pie on a rotating plate in an illuminated case at a restaurant.

19

How do you feel about these woods? she asked. Or perhaps she asked: Do you like living in the forest preserves? One thing that she didn't say and that I didn't intuit at the time was she had been spying on me for the last six months.

How do you like living here? she asked.

Hell, I said. Absolute hell. Although at the time I think I told her the precise opposite. More than words can say.

Do you like these woods? she asked in her way and in my own way I told her I love them.

More than words can say, I said.

Do you like these woods? she asked in her way and in my own way I told her I did.

More than words can say, I said.

We sat a while and she asked the question again as if she weren't sure what I had just said.

So—she said—tell me. Do you like living here?

Where? I asked.

In these woods.

I have no choice but to love them I told her. It's either love them even though in our heart's core we hate them more than words can say or it's hate them as much as our heart's core hates them. To hate them and not love them would be the very defini-tion of hell. I couldn't for a second imagine living in these woods that are the most horrible place imaginable and not trying in my own way to make peace with this place and the way I make peace with these woods is I have trained myself on the level of instinct to love them even though I hate them in my heart's core more than words can say.

Oh, she said in her way listening to me ramble on about my feelings for these woods and it was then when the idea occurred

20

to me that what was really happening to me—if you looked at it objectively, what was happening to me in front of my very own eyes—was I was being taken away from this place. Even though indeed it was my greatest desire indeed to finally be chosen by someone or something and taken away from these woods it was almost a counterinstinct of mine—in fact it was a dangerous instinct—to suspect that someday someone might indeed come for me and take me away from these woods and even though she represented for me a way out of these woods I nevertheless had grave issues with capitulating for I didn't want to become a tchotchke that she put on her shelf after her use for me had run its course. I'm a man I told myself taking another toke from her pot pipe: not some specimen that she on one of her shopping sprees can collect and take home with her and place on her shelf for everyone to see that she had been on an unusual tourist trip of sorts to the far end of the forest preserve road. And look, she might point out if anyone asked: look at what I found on my journey. Isn't this an interesting specimen? she might ask the crowd of visitors gathered about the case as if she were a docent at the Wheeling Historical Society. And where did you collect this specimen? one or another of the observers might ask—with a curiosity and acquisitiveness that was so ferocious as to scare the living daylights out of me. And there she is pointing at me with a stick while I sit like some rumphulus in my case: Would you believe she would say I found him in the local forest preserves living in a hovel a stone's throw from this very spot? While others laughed bravo. Oh impossible to believe, one connoisseur might point out. If that's the case where is the exile's beard? Or another might say: Can you make him howl for us? And then chop chop from my lady and I would howl on command: howl like I meant it

21

as if my insides were being twisted by the very grief this display
in this very comfortable setting, her home, was designed to deny
I suffered. And so I would howl and howl and howl and I would
prance about and moon and mug with my face trying to scare
the yokels and another might point out that I was indeed a very
rare but collectible specimen. This one here, he might point out
with a bit of flourish, is a very notable and rare example of one
of those banished to the woods. For one, he has no beard and
for two he gives off one of the loveliest howls I have ever heard.
Yes! Yes! The howl I agree. The howl is what attracted me to him
in the first place . . . and it went on like this, let me tell you, for
weeks on end. The parties Meredith threw—and always there was
a point in the party where they would all gather round the trophy
case—and this one woman who wore a blue hat and had blue
mascara and claimed she was from Chicago, a connoisseur from
Gallery I don't know what—but how lovely he is this specimen
you've collected. And Meredith was quite overwhelmed with pride
at her acquisition. And how, says this Kate from the Wheeling
Historical Society who couldn't resist tickling my bare foot—trying
to get a rise out of me—and how did you acquire him? And then
the lengthy story told ad nauseam of well, come over here. Let's
step away from the display case for a moment. Let's look out the
window over here. And I came to collect him, Meredith explained,
because there just beyond my yard is the threshold of the woods
and if you train yourself as I have trained myself to peer deep
into the chaos of the woods—which are filled with bugs in summer and leaves and the thicket of a sprawling jungle but in winter
the trees are bare branched and delicate and beautiful—but if
you train yourself to look carefully enough but over time you will
come to see not three hundred yards from our vantage point a

22

rise in the earth and just behind that knoll . . . is our rumphulus's hovel. In short I had acquired him after peering into the woods so long I came to see shapes where I had seen no shapes before in short I had acquired him by training my eyes how to look off into this chaos of birch and bramble and by so looking I had come to see him. And once I had grown used to watching him: learning his ways—his comings and goings—it was simply a matter of reaching out to him when he was most desperate. It was simply a matter of confronting his desperation and just like that he came home with me and ever since he has abided in my house: a rumphulus in a case.

Only this one, said the curator at the Wheeling Historical Society who refused to stop tickling my bare foot, is quite unusual.

And another, a docent of the same society smoking a cigarette and blowing the smoke into my face said, Yes quite so. For this one lacks a beard.

And another an amateur anthropologist said: Whereas the others that are known to have been banished to the woods—the quintessential type so to speak, they all have beards.

And yet this one is clean shaven.

Howl for us honey, Meredith commands. Chop. Chop.

And so I howl and howl and I prance and mug and moon—because one day, I say to myself locked up in that case: you will be abandoned yet again like all things collected are invariably abandoned sooner or later collecting dust & rust &c. So make the most of it, I say to myself, mooning for all that I'm worth. And what a pretty howl it is in her pretty house on the cusp of the forest though to be quite honest her house wasn't pretty at all: there was nothing pretty about it, it was a wreck fallen into dis-

23

repair. It was a scab and blight upon the land. It was a bungalow in ruin and collapse and there I was beneath a bare bulb in her trophy case—soon to be forgotten and soon to be collecting dust: for don't you see I was nothing / I am nothing more than a beard-less rumphulus or worse a tchotchke that she had collected. And how did I become a tchotchke? Well you heard Meredith's story and her story never varied and pretty soon it was her story that achieved ascendency—and no other narrative of what happened was allowed to compete with hers—and so it was patented as undeniable truth. And even the curator at the Wheeling Historical Society wrote about it, and the others who came to bear witness to my antics in the case told their stories, and those who heard the stories of the maiden and the rumphulus retold the story and it was in this fashion that I became lost in a tale that was fueled by rumor and innuendo, succored by myth and fallacy, expanded into an entangling net of misinformation that featured her, Mer-edith, as finder and me, the rumphulus, as found and whereas before these stories had started I was merely a nothing but I was a nothing that I could live with but now with the echoing rever-beration of the stories I was worse than a nothing. I was in point of fact just a rumphulus that jumped at the slightest mention of a stick and gagged and howled and bayed the moon as if I really meant it.

And I was an unusual rumphulus because I was clean shaven while all the others were known to have beards.

No I didn't want that fate at all even though I wanted the fate of being stranded in these godforsaken woods even less. Nevertheless, she saw right through me. She knew more than even I myself knew that I would indeed go home with her and

24

if push came to shove I would agree to be a trophy on her shelf for all to look upon even as I collected dust for being unused and unwanted.

All right then, she says in her way brushing strands of hair from her face. Let's get up and go home. Hey let's go to my place, it's not far from here, why don't we go there.

● ● ● ●

We drove for what seemed like hours though I know it was only a few minutes through the woods. We drove down the long quiet road that leads out of the forest preserves and back into the world that had somehow rebuked me before I even thought I had a chance to be rebuked. Her fingers were long and thin and she had these huge amber rings on each knuckle that reminded me somehow of spiders. I remember thinking how unlikely it was: just how remarkable and unpredictable the world could get sometimes and now here was this woman who seemed entirely too small to be driving this sedan not only driving it but carrying me as if I were her trophy collected at the far terminus of her journey back to her home. Her arms were surprisingly thin and tan and well scrubbed and she wore a white halter top with red lace stitched into the neck and hemline. She kept looking into the rearview mirror and chatted on about old movies. Once in a while she'd say something about a toothache. Then she'd turn and smile at me, smile not like other people smile but smile like only she seemed capable of smiling: out the pit of her eyes her blue eyes seeming like tunnels or search lights or just plain blue like the color of a high summer sky. Flat chalky blue.

As we drove through there, I felt almost like a prisoner being hauled off from his turf as if something personal from deep inside of me were being brought forth into the broad summer light for all to see. I felt terribly terribly exposed and I can't say exactly what that personal thing was only that it was perhaps my deepest desire to leave these woods yet after all of my time living in these woods I had trained myself so thoroughly to love them that leaving them suddenly became the most terrifying thing imaginable. I remember how I wanted to remember everything: how for instance it was a summer day when she came to collect me from my picnic bench at that so-called tourist town that was really just the place where a humble picnic bench sat alongside the river across a green park a stone's throw from her blue Pontiac. Overhead the leaves from the treetops formed a canopy high up in the air. Misconstruing the trees for friends I stuck my hand out the window and reached for the leaves of the overhanging branches to shake them farewell: farewell leaves—I thought to myself as she drove me out of there. Farewell my friends, my trees, I said to myself as she drove me out of there talking about old movies and occasionally about the toothache that she said was bothering her.

My left molar. I can't eat a thing until I get my tooth fixed and I can't get my tooth fixed until I somehow scrape up enough cash. I can't eat a thing because of my tooth and I can't fix my tooth because of this money problem.

Of course at the time I didn't know why she was telling me all of this stuff. At the time I thought she was telling me this stuff because I thought she thought that I and only I was worthy to receive such confessions of hers but later it was obvious to

26

me that had I not been with her in the car that day, had it been someone other than me or even more to the point had she merely been alone in the car by herself she would have nevertheless said the exact same words to herself that she was now telling me.

My tooth is killing me, and there's no fixing it until I fix these money problems.

I thought she was telling me this because she thought I was important enough to hear such personal information but I've now come to see that I was wrong on that point as I was wrong on so many other points.

We drove down the long winding forest preserve road and she nattered on and while she nattered she talked to herself as if she were talking to me. Meanwhile I stopped listening to her altogether and I talked to myself without making any pretense of talking to her. Farewell, I said to myself: farewell each of you, each leaf and tree. Goodbye trees. You are my closest friends, I told myself talking to myself staring deep into the woods as if I were staring into the wide-open eyes of my closest and most vital friend. I have never had a closer nor more vital friend than you, I thought to myself as she pulled me out of there. These twenty-seven months out here living alone so desperately out in these woods—which by the way has been absolute hell—but these twenty-seven months with you has convinced me that despite everything despite all our differences, you, you trees, you are my closest my most vital friends. And it was true. For those twenty-seven months nobody was closer to me than these woods I could recognize nearly every tree: they were familiar to me like old friends and I listened to them carefully trying to hear if they had any final words of farewell for me that day. But I knew they didn't they wanted to get rid of me as much as the world did—that

27

much I was certain of—I loved the woods nevertheless loved them despite the fact that living there those twenty-seven months was absolute hell.

We drove out of there in her blue Pontiac. I don't know how long we drove but at the roadside just as we merged onto the highway I thought I saw Mike there. Standing in the brush. Waving me off. I didn't know then but I know now that it was the last glimpse of the man I would ever have and then he would vanish: what became of him who could say.

Farewell, his wave seemed to say to me. Farewell, Joseph, goodbye and don't come back! Yes it was true. I could see it in his eyes. Farewell, Joseph, whatever you do don't come back.

Farewell, I said back to my great mentor without saying it either by gesture or a parting gaze. Farewell, Mike, I said to myself, and then I added: Until.

Just like that I could almost hear his rebuke.

That is just like you, Joseph, always living with delusions. There will be no more untils.

Well so be it. If I was going to have any delusions it was okay with me and I tried to tell him as much waving goodbye and then of course there was that tug on his beard followed by that nervous look over his shoulder and in a moment he was gone vanished into a dark and impenetrable wilderness that wasn't wilderness at all but just the lousy shithole it really was: the county forest preserves and it was the most miserable place imaginable and even as I escaped a second time in Meredith's Pontiac and to her home, I knew it was only a matter of time before I escaped back into the woods.

I couldn't remain a rumphulus forever.

Part 2
The Woods

I thought back to the beginning. I thought back to the moment when I had first been rebuked—though it had been only twenty-seven months ago yet it seemed a lifetime. Remember I said to myself how when you first stepped into these woods after having been rebuked by the world to feast forty days and forty nights on locusts even though as it turns out it was many more than forty days and nights remember how you felt on the level of instinct the imperative of orienting yourself to these woods in such a way that the woods were construed not as enemies which is what they were but as the dearest friends imaginable?

You're fooling yourself, Mike who in his former life had been a tax collector liked to tell me whenever I told him how much I loved this place. He was always sagacious. But on this point on the point of me fooling myself into believing this place—these woods—was the most wonderful place of all places to be he proved he was sagacious and insightful beyond reproach. I however for reasons of survival was unwilling to concede.

As I say Mike once upon a time in a life long ago had been a tax collector until he like me and all the others had been rebuked by the world. He had been rebuked much earlier than I had been rebuked and so he had been living alone out here in the woods in a small hidden encampment for years possibly a decade or more: oh who knows there's no telling and even he I think can no longer remember a time when he lived anywhere else other than here or was anything else other than a rebuked man hiding from the world in these woods. He certainly only vaguely remembered his former existence as a tax collector if he remembered it at all for you see it quickly became difficult to imagine living anywhere else

31

other than here once you ended up here. It was equally difficult to remember being anywhere else other than here once you were sent here. If you had been rebuked by the world and discharged into this so-called wilderness you never forgot being rebuked but you quickly forgot the time before you were rebuked you quickly forgot living anywhere else other than here or any other existence other than the existence you lived here in these woods, which was an existence founded upon the elemental struggle to survive that was a struggle without reason or cause fomented by something akin to an urge to live such as it was or an urge not to die—a terror of that, of death such as it was.

• • • •

In any event like everyone else stranded out in these woods—people like Adam for instance or that gentle soul Paul who had been a former priest before being caught with child molestation—Mike the tax collector had a small encampment that was so well hid that for all the many months I spent in the woods I never stumbled upon it nor could I ever guess exactly where it was. The same could be said of everyone else that lived out here all of us exiled and abandoned souls we had each learned how to live so discreetly that these woods which comprised no more than five square miles of county park land seemed to each of us effectively empty, barren of any other human soul though there had to be at least twenty and upward of fifty souls depending on the season living day to day in these woods. We lived so discreetly in our well-hid hovels that no one knew precisely where anyone else lived or for that matter how anyone else got by. Sure there were the howls that would burst forth through the night howls that sometimes seemed surprisingly close at hand but despite one's ability to track location by sound even these howls never gave anyone's precise location away. What's more our discretion living in these woods kept us from inquiring with any urgency where one or another of us might be shacked up or how we lived with any precision.

Mike for instance was not inclined to let me know where he was encamped or how he got by day to day just as I was inclined not to ask nor for that matter to tell him where I was encamped or how I got by though I secretly suspect that he knew precisely where in the woods I made my home (as I secretly suspected where in these woods he too might make his home). He also knew how I got by, I'm sure, for we all got by the same way though we pretended not to know how we each got by: hand to mouth and of course there were the dumpsters scattered around town that we perforce were not above visiting and often it was the case visiting one or another of the dumpsters in town that we would bump into one or another of the others rebuked and stranded in these woods and we would look at each other surprised as if to say: what—you mean this is how you get by as well? And we would feign our surprise for in truth there was nothing surprising about it at all. We had to eat after all and barring some hidden stores of cash or food what other way could we be expected to subsist? Hunting and gathering? And yet there was a little of that too: often at night you could smell the scent of roasting squirrel or rabbit or partridge or in some cases from time to time even the scent of roasting venison meat wafted in the air. And even I who prior to being rebuked by the world was the strictest vegetarian imaginable—that's to say I was absolutely an ideological vegan— but out here forced against my will to subsist in ways that I had not psychologically prepared myself for, even I with shock and horror wasn't above hunting and if you hunted in these woods as we were all wont to do from time to time you hunted by snare or net or knife blade or even by stealth, sneaking up on a bird or luring it to your hand with berries and then quickly you would wring its neck. No, I certainly found I wasn't above this type of subsistence and even after a few times of neck wringing I found my squeamishness disappear and I could twist the neck of the small fragile bird and I would listen for the slight gurgle and snapping of bones and I would feel not squeamishness but a certain small joy that this bird had given up its life so that I might carry on another day. And I found myself deeply satisfied with this simple equation that animal x must die so that I animal z could push ahead—stomach full—into another day. Also people weren't above using guns to obtain game so from time to time you could hear a pistol shot ring out and if you heard a pistol shot you knew that either a score was being settled for there was a small amount of murder by gunshot that took place in these woods or as was more often the case you knew that a deer or some form of small game or fowl had been taken down. So though we pretended not to know where we each lived or how we got by, in truth we knew exactly where each hovel was just as certainly as we knew that tomorrow we would be meeting one or another of our kind at the dumpster behind the grocery store or be smelling from the camp just beyond view the strong scent of roasting game.

• • • •

You see these woods, I would say to Mike whenever I saw him pretending indeed that these were woods and not more properly the local forest preserves. We'd be standing on a small trail.

34

I've lived here so long, Joseph, Mike would say, I forget to
see them, he would say only half ironically with a little mournful
note in his voice. Joseph, he would say with a touch of melancholy in his voice: I've been here so long I forget to see that these
woods are woods. I forget to realize, he'd say in his mournful
way, that I spend my whole life out here in the woods. Which is
odd, he would say, because most of the time all I can think about
is how the hell I'll ever get out of this place, even though I know
in my heart of hearts that such thinking is the vainest form of
self-delusion the mind can take out here in this horrible place.

You see these woods, I would say.

Which woods, Joseph, he would say only half ironically.

These woods here.

Ah yes for a moment a brief moment, he would say—a touch
melancholically—I had forgotten them. I had become quite uncon-
scious of them.

Well these woods—

Yes—

They've become for me my closest friends.

Good for you, Joseph, he would say. Not me.

Not you?

For me they remain just some crappy place, which I desperately want to escape, they're the enemy and as soon as I escape
them, I shall very happily forget them and never think of them
again as long as I live.

Not me, I would say a little too emphatically as if I were
trying a little too hard to convince him that such was the case.
Not me, I would say to him. I arrived here hating this place but
since I've been here well I've never felt more at home. Or to put
it another way, I would say to him a little less emphatically: of all

35

the places I've ever been I've never felt more at home than here in these woods, I would tell Mike who also had this nervous tic that made him look constantly over his shoulder as if he were being chased by some malevolent thing.

These woods have become very important to me, I would tell him and I see now just how obnoxious my telling him this was.

I hate them Joseph, he'd say blandly as if he truly hated them.

They're like a friend to me I would say. I feel them as if they're a friend to me.

Stupid, he would say. That's just a stupid thing to say and off he'd go, our time of leisure abruptly coming to an end. He'd go on his way and I'd go on mine.

Until we meet again, I'd say into the woods dashing off in a different direction than he and if he heard me which he invariably did because hearing became acute in the woods he'd say back ever so politely: Until, Joseph.

• • • •

Of course I didn't see then what I see now.

Isn't it interesting I think to myself as I write these notes here in my hovel . . . Isn't it interesting that what we thought we knew deep in our bones proved not to be the case at all? Isn't it interesting, I tell myself more and more these days, that one day we think something to be so absolutely the case that we would stake our mortal souls upon it but with time we inevitably find that everything changes and what was once so certain is now often exactly opposite the case?

Like these woods, for example. I once and for a long time a long period of time I construed them as my friend. What other choice did I have? It was a matter of life and death to see these woods as being my most important ally in all the world. But now I see—and time has forced me to see this—that I had misconstrued these woods as my friend and that in point of fact these woods were never my friend at all I can see that now but it wasn't always the case. Once and for a long time I was deeply infatuated with the woods and I never thought for the life of me I would ever overcome this infatuation.

But Mike, to his credit, whenever we would meet wandering our own separate ways through the woods but Mike could instantly see through me. He could see that what I had misconstrued as a true friend, the woods, was merely my infatuation with the place.

You're kidding yourself, he liked to tell me whenever I brought up how happy I was living in the very bosom of my friend, the woods. You're kidding yourself if you think this place is your friend. Trust me on this, you might not see it now, but you will. This place is no friend of yours. He'd look quickly over his shoulder to see if anyone was sneaking up on him and without saying so much as another word he'd be gone dashing off in one direction or another through the woods and I knew I'd do well to dash off in any direction other than the direction Mike was headed in.

I understood Mike in that regard. He lived in the woods. He hated it. If we happened to meet we'd exchange vital information or if we had more leisure we'd discuss anything under the sun but when it got to be too much, when our leisure time suddenly became oppressive to one or another of us or to both of us as happened from time to time, off we'd dash through the brambles and brush making a getaway and the way either of us dashed off suggested to the other whether we wanted to be followed or not.

Mike would say occasionally without actually saying it that I should follow him, and off he'd dash and he'd say it merely by the way he dashed off that I should follow him and so I would. We were both very agile in the woods. We could move nearly as quickly as the white-tailed deer that lived in these woods moved. We could move with agility with grace with alarming speed ducking and dodging through the impenetrable maze of brush brambles and close clustered trees. It was amazing to me and I never lost that sense of amazement how quickly one became situated to life in the woods: how all the old reflexes honed over thousands of generations of living in the woods, how those old reflexes that were developed precisely for survival in the woods but it always amazed me how quickly those old reflexes quickly ascended to the fore and took over. And of course there was the oldest reflex of all, which was the inescapable reflex to persevere, to survive, which was crazy really because in my heart of hearts there were times whole months would slip by and during those months I wished with all my soul to be done with it.

Sitting overlooking the river, Mike and I would talk about how we hated to live like this and how there were days we woke up and wished for nothing more than to go back asleep and never wake again.

If I should die before I wake, Mike would say, I would be happy. But I don't want to die here and I wouldn't know how to die anywhere else, so I'm cursed to carry on.

We all had our reasons for carrying on.

I should like to die myself, I would tell Mike when I was feeling bleak in my heart's core, but I always think—I would tell Mike sitting on that bench—what if my luck turns around tomorrow? I can't bear the thought of ending it all only days before my luck turns: like being killed in a war the day before the war ends.

Yes, that would suck, Mike would say. Always felt sorry, he would say, for the poor bastards killed on Armistice Day.

Likewise, I would say, to die when the war was already over. To die while one was already in view of home would be the most ignominious thing imaginable.

In this way we managed to divert ourselves.

I carry on, Mike says from time to time when we're staring at the river flowing by, because I feel I don't have a choice.

I suppose I carry on, I would say echoing Mike's sentiment, because I don't have a choice either. What other choice is there? Death?

There's that choice, yes.

I agree but I don't have the heart to do myself in.

Nor me.

And so we carry on.

Yes.

But in truth I didn't know why I carried on especially when I was feeling bleak in my heart's core with no clear escape in sight. I suppose I carry on, I would say to my self all alone in my hovel feeling sick at heart, because I feel I really don't have a choice. I would say to myself—I carry on out of habit.

Or a will to live, Mike would say, looking over his shoulder because of that nervous tic of his or if he wasn't looking over his shoulder he was forever running his fingers through his beard which was a dark black beard unruly and unshaved.

You should shave, I would say to him.

39

You should mind your own business.

For in truth there were two kinds of people locked up in these woods, that's how I saw it at least: there were those who let their beards grow and there were those, I among them, who were very finicky about our appearance.

If you ever want to leave this place, I would tell Mike from time to time, you would do well to shave.

Mind your own business, he would say with a bitterness that made me laugh.

Only trying to help, I would say.

Well you're not helping, you're hurting. He'd tug at his beard, look quickly over his shoulder and off he'd go disappearing into the brambles and brush making no sign that I should follow.

Until next time, I would say off in my direction and in the distance a voice surprisingly delicate and beautiful and forgiving would respond,

Until, Joseph.

. . . .

If you want to escape these environs, I would tell Mike from time to time.

What environs?

These woods.

Yes, what do you recommend?

Shave.

Leave my beard out of it.

I'm only trying to help.

Help nothing. This is more harm than good, believe me.

If you want to leave these environs and enter back into the

40

world, I would say trying my best to be of some help to him, you would do well to look like those who live out there. You would do well to shave and not look like Grizzly Adams.

Grizzly who?

You know who I'm talking about.

See you, he would say. I've had enough. Tug on his beard, a nervous look over the shoulder and off he'd go in a way that suggested I better not follow.

Until—I would say and in a surprisingly beautiful and delicate voice echoing through the woods back at me would be his voice full of forgiveness saying the words,

Until, Joseph.

● ● ● ●

Yes I would say. That's it. The pesky will to live looking over my shoulder too because that tic always made me look nervously over my shoulder then off we'd go our separate ways. Him seeing his plight eye to eye. And me forever fooling myself.

● ● ● ●

Other times we would meet at the crossroads of one trail or another and I would tell him that these woods were like a friend to me: it was an uncontrollable urge I had to try to convince him how much I loved being here locked up in this so-called wilderness.

He'd laugh derisively whenever I brought it up.

You're fooling yourself, he'd say, looking over his shoulder because of that nervous tic of his. He would say: you only think

41

these woods are your friends, but what you don't realize is that in point of fact these woods are your enemies. You would do well to get out of here as soon as possible and never think of them again as long as you live.

Nonsense, I would say laughing. Of everyone I have ever known I have never known anyone so understanding of me as these woods appear to be. I feel utterly at home here.

When I leave this place, he would say, I would like to never remember them as long as I live.

* * * *

Sometimes when we ran into each other, I'd say to him:
See these woods?
Which woods?
These woods.
Oh yes. I've lived here so long I forget sometimes to realize that I live here out among the trees. I forget the trees so they become invisible to me. It's a survival mechanism, no doubt. It's my way of persevering, no doubt. My greatest desire is to leave these woods. I've found that if I can't leave them bodily, then I can at least train my mind not to notice them.
You see these woods?
No.
Look. Look. I would say.
Ah yes. Now I see them. He'd tug on his beard look over his shoulder that nervous tic of his and then he'd be gone on his way.

Or other days: see these woods?

Yes, of course I see them. Most terrible place in the world. How could I not see them?

They are, I mean these trees here, these trees are like my closest friends in the world. I've become I feel as if these trees are closer to me than any human being with the exception of my mother has ever been. These trees, I would tell him, are to me the closest friend imaginable.

I hate the sight of them, he would say bitterly.

They are the most beautiful friends I have ever had. I have learned tremendous life lessons from them.

I hate the sight of them, he'd say.

I've learned how to stay put. These trees have taught me a lesson: how to stay put. Everything is in motion—the cars on the highways the airplanes overhead but these trees and the earth they're rooted to have taught me an incredibly vital lesson— the lesson of staying put. It's the most vital lesson I have ever learned.

It's a lesson, he would point out, you should forget if you ever want to get out of this place, he'd say. But if you're like me and desperately want to get out of here, it's a lesson you'd do well never to take to heart.

I feel as if these woods are a friend of mine, don't you see? I would say to him.

You're fooling yourself, he'd say. You're still young and dumb. These woods aren't your friend. When are you going to wake up and realize that? These woods are the enemy and you'd do well to forget you ever lived here.

43

Other times he'd say to me: My advice to you . . . Tug at his beard. Look over his shoulder, that nervous tic. My advice to you, partner, he'd say, is get over your infatuation with these woods as soon as you can. They are no friend of yours. They are your worst misfortune and the sooner you realize this the better. Then he'd go off on his way and I'd go off on mine and my direction was always a different direction from his of late and off I'd go dashing into the dark brambles saying the word: Until, which was my custom, and he, as was his custom, would throw his voice toward me saying with an incredible note of forgiveness: Until, Joseph, and I knew by his saying that we wouldn't see each other for a very long time because one thing you learned while living out in these woods was how to avoid above all being seen. You learned how to remain inviolate and hidden for as long as you so choose. And during those days we all chose to remain more often than not inviolate and hidden from each other for long periods of time trying to manage in our own way the twin anxiety of both being here which was the most horrible place imaginable and leaving here which we all deeply wished for yet feared with an anxiety that was so large it was barely manageable. All day long and night time too one dealt continually with the anxiety of entering back into the rebuking world and when one could no longer contain one's anxiety a howl inarticulate and gasping would burst forth from one's inner core and you could hear it through the woods: a whole pack of wolves howling to each other, only these weren't wolves but the insuppressible howls of rebuked men screaming in agony trying to control the unmanageable anxiety that sometimes incarnated as an uncontrollable howl.

．．．．

Within minutes of entering into these woods for the first
time and before I had ever met Mike—hi hi his hand up in the
air—that mournful baleful look in his eye that told me in so many
words: you're too young to have been sent here, your life is too
long to be doomed like this. But within those first few moments
of being in these woods I realized that I had to try, as much
as possible, to take a constructive approach to being here. For
instance, I told myself, you might try to learn every tree over
say a six-inch diameter in these woods and so, almost immediately, I made it my task to recognize all the trees greater than
a six-inch-trunk diameter in these woods. Before long and it
didn't take that very much time either, I came to recognize nearly
every tree in this godforsaken place that as Mike so adamantly
pointed out and which I knew in my heart truly was a godforsaken place even though I, for matters of self-preservation, was
unwilling or unable—as the case may be—to see. For matters of
self-preservation I began training myself almost immediately to
love these woods as if they were my happy home as if each tree
that these woods were comprised of were for me among my best
friends in all the world. As a result I had come to see each tree
not as a tree but as a unique individual with a personality of
sorts all its own. Each tree became for me an individual and each
tree was a friend and before long—and as I say it happened with
surprising speed my reflexes coming to the fore and the strongest
of all my reflexes being the will to survive—I felt compelled on
some deeply biological level to recognize every tree in this pseudo
wilderness as if that tree were the most vital friend in all the
world to me. Each tree became familiar as old friends and they

were all old friends before I knew it and I listened to each tree and to all of the trees very carefully. Upon entering the woods that first time it occurred to me that these trees and these woods by extension might have something to tell me so I taught myself how to listen to the trees which wasn't a very difficult thing at all to teach myself. And I would sit swaying in the upper branches of one tree or another for long periods of time listening to the chorus of trees around me, which whispered or sang or spoke as the wind blew and they would speak in concert or discord depending on how the wind blew and if it was stormy they would quite naturally speak discordantly and if it was calm and peaceful the trees spoke a different message entirely.

For matters of self-preservation alone I allowed myself to be lulled by the intoxicating beauty of the place and by the voices of the trees even though, objectively, if you looked at it very carefully there was nothing very beautiful at all about being stranded out here in this godforsaken place. But I allowed myself to see these woods not for what they were (the county forest preserves) but for what they—in point of fact—were not: the most important and beautiful friends I've ever had. For reasons that I can only describe as the biological urge to survive, I had taught myself, and it was the hardest thing in all the world to do, I had taught myself to see these woods as being home sweet home even though these woods were in point of fact the wasteland that I had been forcibly discharged into upon being rebuked by the world. The only reason I was here, I would say to myself from time to time in rare moments of truth, is not because I chose to be here of my own volition but because I had no choice. I've been forcibly rebuked by the world don't forget, I would tell myself. Whatever you do, I would tell myself in rare moments of self-awareness, never forget that you have been forcibly rebuked by the world and the reason you are here is because this wasteland at the edge of civilization was the only place left to which I could be discharged. These woods, therefore, were in effect a prison of sorts. But like all prisoners I had to learn at an almost biological level—and I realized this within moments of stepping into these woods—that if I wanted to continue to exist then I must somehow figure out how to construe these woods as the most beautiful and necessary friends in all the world. I had to construe at some deep level as if I were reengineering my most native instincts—which when I first came out here were horrified by this place—but I had to construe at the level of instinct that this was indeed a sort of paradisiacal place and that no other place I have ever been to or seen could even remotely compare to the wonders of this godfor-saken and horrible place.

I don't think I've ever known another human being, I would tell Mike when I ran into him that first time and upon each subse-quent visit that I ever had with him: I don't think I've ever known another human being whom I have loved more than these woods. Of course it was all a charade my saying this but to Mike's credit and again need I point out that Mike was among the most saga-cious fellows abandoned to live out his days in these woods, but Mike's sagacity—his wisdom—allowed him to see what my instincts upon being reengineered refused me at first glance to see: that I was in point of fact living a lie indeed the opposite was the case. These woods were the enemy or to put it another way, these woods couldn't care less about me whether I lived or died didn't make a hill of beans of difference to these woods. Why should they care what became of me? If I lived so be it. If I died so be it. Either case was of the smallest imaginable concern to these

47

woods. These woods had other things to worry about and I was the least of all the things they had to worry about. My little problems were the least important things in all the world for these woods to worry about that's what made me love the woods—their *indifference*! That's what I told myself, at least, and I clung as long as I could to this charade as if it were a palpable truth that could save me.

I love this place, I would tell him even though I was miserable beyond belief in my heart's core.

You're kidding yourself, he would say. Or he would tell me to tell my mother someday that I love these woods more than her. Tell your mother, he would say, and see what she says about your abiding love for this godforsaken place.

I love them more than any human being, I would tell Mike, with the exception of my mother whom I love without condition.

You're lucky to have her.

Lucky isn't the word. But these woods . . .

Stop bringing it up. I hate the place and can think of nothing more I'd rather do than leave it for good. I certainly don't want to talk about it.

And then because I was so young and insensitive I would tell him point blank: you'll never leave these woods, I'd say to him from time to time with maximum cruelty just to upset him.

You'll never leave this place, I'd say. No matter what you may think or hope, it's hopeless, don't you see? You'll never, ever leave this place.

What are you, nuts? he'd say, outraged beyond belief. Those words you just spoke, you may think them but don't ever say them. You're messing with fire.

I'm just telling the truth, I'd say innocently.

48

Say any truth under the sun, but never say that truth.

But if I omit one truth then who knows—a river of falsehoods will flood through the dam.

Never, no matter what you do, never tell it like that. You can think it, even believe it, he would say to me, but never tell it. Ok?

What?

Never say that I'll never leave these woods. Do you know, he would say to me tugging at his beard and looking over his shoulder that nervous tic of his that he'd never been able to overcome. Do you know that the most casual words can sometimes be the most deadly? So be careful of what you say out here lest you or worse I come to no good over it.

And then later we'd meet again and he'd say: you almost killed me with those words you said to me back then.

Which words are those?

You know which. That I would never leave these woods. Don't you realize, he'd say. The most casual words can be more deadly than gunfire. You should watch what you say.

Sorry, I told him. I had no idea.

Those words of yours, I needn't tell you, but I will. Those words of yours have hung over me like a curse. I hate this place and can think of nothing more I'd rather do than leave it.

Well good luck to you in your endeavors.

It's not so easy, you see, he'd say.

You're telling me.

I hate these woods and fear I'm going to die in them. Such a death would be ignominious to me. Who should care whether I live or die? No one really. There isn't a soul in the world who would care whether I live or die, he would say in his mournful but deeply sagacious manner, but I care. Don't you see, even though

49

no one else cares what becomes of me whether I leave these fucking woods or not whether I die today or live another, I care. It means something to me. It's a goal of mine to survive.

It's our instinct.

Yes, he'd say. You're very right about that. It's our self-preservation instinct. But your saying I'm never going to get out of here, no matter how true that may be, is tantamount to killing me. Your saying those words—you're never going to get out of here, are the most deadly words that can be spoken out here and you must cease and desist at once.

I understand, I would say shocked at the force of his passion.

You may not care whether I live or die, whether I'll escape or no, and I don't presume that you should. But I care. God knows no one else cares what becomes of me, and again, I don't presume to think they should. In fact, there are people in the world, let me tell you, who secretly wish that I would perish out here all alone, but if I died out here, I don't presume that anyone would leastwise give a damn. In fact, for this silly instinct to persevere I wouldn't give a damn either, tell you the truth. But then, should I die, I'd feel somehow as if I'd let myself down.

I understand, I would say, believe me.

If I should die out here alone, no one on earth would care. The fact is, if I died out here, I would die like so many dead deer that die out here alone in the woods, I'd just become another decaying carcass disintegrating somewhere out here into the earth.

Dust to dust, ashes to ashes, I would say to Mike whenever we happened upon the corpse of a moldering deer.

Need more be said than that?

It's the cycle of life. We live we die we molder and there it is: one day next season we're just flints of bone hidden in the green grass.

It's an ignominious way to die. I should not like to perish like all the other animals perish out here. I should not like to be roadkill. I should like to think my life has more value than that, he would say in his mournful way, but then again, I don't presume that I'm any better than the other wild animals stranded in this godforsaken place, and like them I don't harbor any illusions that I'll end up any differently: being nothing more significant than roadkill.

Oh surely you're better than common roadkill, I would say— and later in my lean-to desperate to figure a way out of this place I'd say to myself in moments of truth: you're kidding yourself to think you're any better than all the animals killed along the roadside, better than these beautiful deer who, when they die, are left in the spot they died in to decay into nothing with the seasons.

You may believe I'm kidding myself to believe I'm no better than the common skunk, but I believe, nevertheless, that I'm better than the common skunk—all kidding aside, he would say. I'm certainly better than the common skunk.

How better? I would ask.

I am a man for chrissakes.

Or other times he'd say this: I'm better because I was born better and I intend to die better too. And then that look over his shoulder and off he was on his way through the brush indicating by the slightest of gestures that I shouldn't follow.

Until next time, I'd say over my shoulder as I plunged ahead

51

on my own direction through the brambles and brush. And then barely audible I'd hear rise on the evening air his most beautiful and delicate voice:

Until.

* * * *

And so it went. I loved the woods even though in my heart's core I hated them and he in his heart's core hated these woods and knew he'd never leave them even though it was his deepest wish to do exactly that.

If you want to leave these woods, I would tell him whenever the idea came upon me.

Let's not bring this up again, he'd warn.

No seriously, I'd say. What's to prevent you from shaving your beard cleaning yourself up immolating your camp and stepping back into the world. What's to stop you from picking up and doing what you claim is your deepest most devout hope: leaving this place.

He'd listen as patiently as he could under the conditions and even from time to time he would try to respond to my question as judiciously as possible. That's a good point, he'd say scratching his beard looking over his shoulder then darting off into some incredibly dense thicket of brambles and brush.

Or if he had the courage not to be evasive as was sometimes the case, he'd say, I like that idea you had right now. The idea of immolating my camp. Never occurred to me before, just that way: immolation. Do you know, he would say to me pulling a cigarette out and lighting it with the flick of a Zippo. There are days on end I sit in my hovel and I wonder how all of this will end. Need I say,

I'd do anything or give anything at all to get out of this godfor-saken and evil place. However, until that thing that I must give in order to get out of here is made clear to me, I'm afraid I don't know exactly how to go about getting out of here.

There are days, he would say from time to time, I try to use my imagination and see into the future with clear and unclouded eyes. What will become of me? I ask myself, he says to me from time to time. What will become of this camp? I ask myself. And sometimes, I swear to god, I can just barely see what may become of it if the worst happens: if I never leave this place and end up like so much roadkill, even though to end up as roadkill would be the most ignominious and terrible way for me to go. I imagine what will become of my camp, my body moldering inside of it, the elements and wind tearing it down shingle by shingle until it too is nothing more than debris moldering in the high grass. But now that you mention it, now that you use that word, *immola-tion*, a whole new idea occurs to me. Had you not used that word immolation, I might have had to face the unsatisfying conclusion that I just laid out for you. But now that the word immolation is in play, I can imagine a different outcome entirely. A more satis-fying outcome. I can imagine the whole thing going up in flames, which is something I've never been able to imagine before. I can imagine with some satisfaction that my hovel—and these woods by extension—will go up in one great conflagration and instead of being roadkill like the common skunk, or the moldering carcass of a dead animal, I'll become instead, a sacrifice immolated by the purifying flames fueled by the shingles of my own despicable hovel. For truthfully, he would say with the greatest sagacity, if you think about it a moment: isn't this rebukement that has been done to us a form of sacrifice?

53

How so, I would ask, trying to follow him—which was sometimes as difficult in conversation as it was literally following him
through the thicket of brambles and brush.

Sometimes it occurs to me, he would say, that the world
doesn't care one way or another what becomes of us out here,
just as it didn't care one way or another what became of us while
we were living our lives—me as a tax collector so many years
ago and you, god knows what the hell you did before you were
rebuked and sent out here—but maybe the whole point of our
being rebuked by the world . . .

You mean there's a point to all this, I would say trying not to
laugh at the hilarity of what this most sagacious of all wise men
was trying to tell me.

Why else be rebuked if not for a point, he'd say with the
utmost seriousness.

And what would that point be?

This is what I think, he would say. We've been rebuked so
that the world can go on, purged of us, purified, so to speak, of
its least desirable elements. That's to say, he'd say, if you look at
it in a certain light, if you have the courage, as I this very minute
do, to look at it—this whole rebukement and strandedness in the
wilderness—if you look at it in a certain light, we have been sacrificed by the world so that the world can carry on, purified of its
most undesirable elements, and therefore cleansed of us. So your
idea of immolation—of self-immolation, if you will—is just one
step closer to completing that cycle of sacrifice and purification.

Or, I would say, trying to take the opposing view. Or, you
could look at it like this: that your whole theory is a bunch of
rot—that there is no point at all in all of this. You could look at it,
if you so choose, if you truly had courage you could look at it like

this: that in all this mess there is no point whatsoever. You could, if you so choose, see that we were rebuked not because of any deficient properties inherent in us but because we happened to be in the wrong place at the right time. That's all. Sorry, you could construe the world as saying to us when it rebuked us. Nothing personal. In fact there's nothing at all wrong with you whatsoever the world might have said to us upon our rebukement and being sent out here in the wilderness forty days and nights to feast on locusts. Nothing personal in all this you are in fact perfectly fine. I rebuke you only because you happened to be in the wrong place at the right time and I was put in a position by virtue of who I am to rebuke you and cast you forth into the wilderness. You see, the world might have said, I have no other choice me being the world other than to rebuke you forever into that little crust of wilderness at the outskirts of our little orderly civilization to feast on locusts or anything else you may be able to get your grubby hands on some forty days and nights or some other time indeterminately if not indefinitely longer than that.

Or you could say, he would say, trying to force me to see his point: you could say that there is a pattern and reason for all this. That it isn't so random.

You could if you were disposed to say so. Or if you were not so disposed you could say so anyway though to do so would be no different than falling in love with these woods while in your heart's core you hate it beyond comprehension.

If there's a pattern, he would carry on, then immolation would make sense. Wouldn't it? If there's reason we've been rebuked and sent out here and there was no chance of escaping this hateful place, even though it's my deepest desire to do so, if we come to recognize our plight for what it is, rebuked by the world for very specific reasons so that it might purge itself of its undesirable elements; and if, once rebuked, there was no path back out into the world that we could discover no matter how carefully we search the footways of these woods for such a path, then the option of self-immolation becomes, thanks to you and your insight, an absolutely satisfying way to end this story. Suddenly he'd scratch his beard look over his shoulder and off with a quickness and sprightliness more rabbit-like than human. He'd be gone leaving the option of his own self-immolation out there on the table for everyone to see.

• • • •

Other times we would meet in the woods and we'd fall back into the same old routine: hand up hi hi and how I love these woods above anything else in the world even though in my heart's core I hated them and was unable to or unwilling to as the case may be admit up front to myself or to Mike just how much in my heart's core I hated this place and yearned above all else to escape this wilderness and enter back into the rebuking world.

First the world rebuked us, I would say, as if exchanging the lightest of gossip even though these were grave and mortally devastating facts, and then, if we live here long enough, we come to love these woods more than anything anyone or any other place on earth, and then we are faced with the issue of how to deal with our desire to leave this place even though it's that thing— leaving these woods—that we have at least in word desired more than anything in the world.

You apparently, he would say putting a cigarette in his mouth or a blade of grass between his lips, desire it less than I do. It's the only thing I desire, escaping these woods. I desire it as a monomaniacal madman obsessed with one object and only one object desires that object. I desire it beyond words or expression. To leave these godforsaken woods is in fact all I am. When you see me at these crossways of the footpaths as we run into each other from time to time you see Mike a former tax collector who's been in these woods an infinite amount of time, but when you look at me what you are really seeing, he would say to me, is one thing and one thing alone: an obsession to leave these woods. A desire so great I can't communicate it. I am, he would say, I am an inarticulate urge to escape these woods, nothing more nor less.

You are also, I would point out, a former tax collector.

I am a former tax collector, he would say, like a possum by the trees of evolution is a snake, or a man is a mouse or an acorn for that matter is the ovum of the most primitive fern. That's to say, he would say, I'm a tax collector in theory only and the remotest theory at that. I'm a tax collector so far back my memory retains only the title tax collector as a descriptive metonym for some guy remotely related to me who in blue blazers and pin-striped suits shod in wing-tipped shoes rambled around town once upon a time briefcase in hand knocking on the doors of tax scofflaws. The reality is I am no longer that and from the moment I was rebuked by the world I've been only an inarticulate urge to escape more deeply and thoroughly and for such an eternity of time that I have become it and it has become I. He would scratch his beard, look nervously over his shoulder and indicating by body language alone whether I should let him go off alone or follow him as the case may be, off he'd go dashing through a thicket of brambles and brush so impenetrable and dense it amazed me even at this late point in my tenure in these woods that a human his

57

size—six four a hundred ninety pounds—could manage somehow
or another to penetrate them with a stealth and quietness that
was breathtaking to behold. And then I because of his nervous tic
would look over my shoulder and off as if I had somewhere to go
I'd dash in the opposite direction or after him as the case may be
and if I did dash off after him I invariably chose a less direct and
more roundabout method of following him not cutting through
the brambles but moving along a ravine that circled beyond the
brambles and—with senses attuned and an ever-growing ability to
track—I could follow him with nearly perfect precision going where
ever he went but by less direct and more convoluted methods.

You follow me, he would say—from time to time when I
followed him—the same way you think. You avoid the rough spots
but despite your more circuitous routes you arrive nevertheless at
the exact spot you're supposed to arrive at.

So what are you saying? I'd ask him.

What I'm saying is there's still hope for you.

How so?

There's still hope that one day you may see that these woods
are anything but your friend. You may end up seeing that these
woods are the worst enemy you ever had and that leaving them
should be your number one priority.

• • • •

But the way he said this his baritone voice rising through the
scale of his words in such a way that what he said was nearly
an incomprehensible and uncontainable howl that reverberated
through the grassy meadow we had been standing in and echoed
far into the green dark and impenetrable woods. And further

58

along deep into the woods the echo of his howl merged with
the reverberating echo of other howls and soon the woods were
charged with the sounds of men screaming at the top of their
lungs in rage or pain or as an expression of shock and dismay at
what ill fortune had befallen them—rebuked and discarded into
this little crust of wilderness as if we were all useless and worthless trash or as Mike liked to point out: as if we were the impuri-
ties that the world by rebuking us purged from its system.

• • • •

Other times Mike and I would meet and he'd be overcome
with a melancholy that was so unbearable he could hardly lift his
hand hi hi our standard operating procedure.

Hi hi I'd say my hand going up in the air.

Hey, he'd say in return. Barely audible, melancholic beyond
belief.

Then he'd dash off in another direction and I wouldn't see him
for many days.

• • • •

Or he wouldn't dash off. He'd stand across from me rubbing
his finger through his beard staring at me as if I were some sort
of shocking revelation, something he'd never expected to see or
stumble upon in his lifetime.

What are you doing here? he'd ask confused for this was
during the period of his great depression.

Same thing as you, I'd say. I've been rebuked and cast off by
the world and so I make my way in this horrible wilderness, which

has become for me the most loving and understanding friend imaginable.

Friend? Mike asked. He looked over his shoulder then turned to me. What friend?

This friend. This wilderness here. This wilderness we're stranded in.

What wilderness are you talking about? he'd ask a little confused.

Why this wilderness of course. Look around you, Mike. Look at all these trees can't you see them?

Oh yes, he'd say, slightly startled, of course I see them. Desire nothing more than escaping them.

And if there was time and nothing pressing for him or me to do I would ask him to tell me about his desire to escape and he would say: Joseph, let me tell you . . . I have wished from the moment I was sent here to leave this place. But slowly, and I don't know how to explain it, but slowly I've come to realize that even though I wish to leave these woods more than a person can desire anything, nevertheless, with the passage of time, I'm beginning to wonder if escaping this place is something that's really going to happen or if it's just a strange illusion that helps sustain me day to day.

Nothing wrong with illusions, I tell him.

There are worse things than illusions.

You think so? And he would smile at me with a touch of that old wisdom that sagacity glinting from his eyes. We all live with illusions.

But to live with the illusion that you're going to escape this place when the reality is you shall never escape this place is per-haps to live with the most dangerous illusion imaginable.

It's an illusion all of us who live here, all of us rebuked, we all live with this illusion. But the thing is, I would tell Mike, trust me. It's not an illusion. I promise you one day we will get out of this place.

You think so, do you?

It's not a question of what I think. It's a reality.

At which point he'd start laughing as if I were the craziest person he'd ever met.

Tell me, Mike would ask. If you're so goddamn sure we're going to escape this place one day, tell me, how do you propose it will happen?

Well for one, I keep shaved. What's more I bathe myself regularly.

And you think this is your ticket out of this place?

Of course I do and you would do well to follow my lead on this issue.

Why? Because it's worked so well for you? he would laugh.

Well no, it hasn't worked for me yet, but I'm closer than ever to escaping these woods.

Tell me, how are you any closer to escaping these woods than I?

Well for one who knows but perhaps someone will come searching for me and finding me take me away from here.

And who would that person be?

I don't know. It's only a premonition. It's hard to explain.

In the meantime you're stuck here like everyone else, and, as far as I can tell, you're no closer to getting out of here than even the most stranded of us.

I disagree with that.

You disagree because you live with illusions. The fact is none

61

of us are ever getting out of here. If leaving this place were as simple as you say—if all one had to do was shave and bathe—then we'd all be clean cut and ready to go. But the fact is, I was clean cut and ready to go when the world for reasons I don't completely understand rebuked me. I was already dressed in a suit. I was wearing wingtip shoes. I was carrying a briefcase. I was working twelve-hour days and making a six-figure salary. I was doing everything exactly by the book, and then, for reasons that I am unable to explain, the world, inexplicably and quite out of the blue rebuked me and sent me here. I don't understand why I was sent here, nor do I know how to escape this horrible place. These two questions, by the way—why I was sent here and how do I get out of here—are the only questions I allow myself to grapple with. At first, I spent more time trying to figure out why I was sent here, but as it proved—to my surprise—to be increasingly difficult to get out of here, I found myself concentrating less on why I was sent here, and more on how to get the hell out of this place. Indeed, the question: how to get out of here is such a pestering and nagging question, such a difficult puzzle to solve that sometimes I believe I may never solve it. All of a sudden, when it occurs to me that a solution to the question: how to get out of here, may be beyond my powers to cogitate, I feel a grim terror take hold of me. If I can't get out of here, I tell myself, then I'm permanently stuck here and if I'm permanently stuck here then I'll never so long as I live leave these horrible and godforsaken woods. In which case I'm doomed to die like so many animals die, worthless and alone, my bones moldering to dust in the high grass. It's our fate, don't you see. We're never getting out of here. But you, Joseph, obviously think that you have solved the puzzle. You obviously believe that leaving this place is as simple as keeping well groomed. You tell me that if I shave my beard and put myself in order—if I try to resemble the people on the outside—that I'll increase my chances of escaping this place. You tell me that by growing this beard and leaving it unruly, I am in effect so much as admitting that contrary to what I say—that I am singularly obsessed with leaving this place—in point of fact I have given up all hope of ever leaving this place. But what you don't seem to see—what you seem incapable of understanding, Joseph, is that no matter what I do I am permanently stuck in this place. It has become increasingly clear to me that if I live to a hundred or if I should die very soon or at least sooner than I thought I might die before my rebukement took place . . . because this rebukement has severely limited my life term . . . then every single day left in me will be spent here in these woods. The reason this has become clear to me—and it's a reason you don't seem able to grasp—is that, from before I was rebuked by the world, I was one of them. I was exactly the person you say I should now model myself upon, and in being that person, in living my role as diligently as possible, I nevertheless was rebuked—mid furrow so to speak. The horse was pulling the plow, I was mid furrow and no sooner did I say, Hi, I am Mike Smith of the IRS and I've arrived here today to discuss tax forms you filed three years ago . . . no sooner did I say these words that were the words I as a respected participant on the outside world was expected to say, no sooner did I say these words than the world suddenly took a strange turn and I was rebuked; and I tell you, I was rebuked with a force and aggression that astonished me, continues to astonish me these nine long years later, leaves me here this moment still standing in shock at the ferocity of my rebukement. I was rebuked and cast off into this shitty little wilderness, and unlike you . . . unlike you

63

I didn't have a guide when I came here. I didn't step into these woods and have someone raise a hand and tell me hello the way I was there for you. Unlike when you arrived there wasn't a community in these woods of the rebuked. I—I'll have you know—was the first of all of us sent here into this wilderness. And it was the hardest and most painful thing imaginable and ever since that day I stepped in these woods I made a vow to myself to leave them as soon as possible and reestablish my place in the world—but slowly, and it's taken an incredible amount of time, but slowly I'm starting to see that my dream of one day leaving this place is just that, a dream. It'll never happen.

I'm sorry to hear that, I would say. I'm sorry you feel that way, Mike.

What's worse, I hate this place so much it makes me sick. Sick as if my insides have been absolutely broken. Just then, he started to sob, so his shoulders shook. He stood there sobbing and stared at me quite nakedly through his tears and not knowing what else to do I did only what I knew how to do. I told him how I felt.

Not me, I love this place.

Ha. Ha. Ha. He laughed through his tears. Now you're trying to make me feel better with your jokes.

I love this place more than anything in the world.

Stop making me laugh. He was sobbing and laughing at the same time.

And unlike you, I tell him. I'm getting out of here. And I hear what you're saying but you would do well to follow my lead and clean yourself up. I'm telling you. It'll help you in your prospect of one day leaving these environs.

Mike always used to tell me you're kidding yourself if you think some person is going to come out of nowhere to rescue you.

You may think I'm kidding, I would tell Mike whenever we got on the subject of my strange premonition that I was going to be taken out of these woods.

You know what, I would tell Mike whenever we ran into each other and had time to talk.

Tell me.

I feel sometimes as if I'm not doomed to spend the rest of my days stranded out here in these woods.

It was a statement that always made Mike laugh in a full-throated sort of way. I'd say: I feel as if someone will one day rescue me, and he'd tilt his head back and his beard at this time was just magnificent and he seemed larger than life and full of sagacity and he'd start laughing this full-throated laugh.

I feel as if sooner or later someone will arrive to take me away from here.

Laugh. The full-throated laugh. His beard and eyes laughing.

I'm serious. It's a premonition I have and I share it with you because I feel I can trust you with such premonitions.

Ha. Ha. Ha. He laughs some more: that tremendous black beard, his tongue gagging at the back of his throat.

You may laugh, I tell him regretting almost immediately having shared my secretest emotion with him, but your laughter doesn't disprove my premonition.

You're right. My laughter disproves nothing, and trust me, he would say, I've discovered that there's nothing I can do or say that would change your mind because you refuse to see things as they are. You are so hell-bent on seeing things as they might be or as you wish they would be that you are unable to see things as they are.

And how are they? I would ask him from time to time and in the most sagacious manner imaginable he would tell me that these woods that we occupied were not only ignominious to an incalculable degree but no matter how much we hoped or wished to do so, we would never again escape them. We're here for life, he would point out, or to be blunt about it, because apparently you require me to be absolutely blunt about this most horrible of truths: we are here for death, until we die. Our life terms here, cut short.

· · · ·

Listen, I would say and there we were sitting in the tall grass of some meadow located deep in the woods and from the woods could be heard the twittering and piping of birds and occasionally the way they talked to each other as if they truly had something urgent to say to each other reminded me of the way we talked to each other.

You and I, I would tell Mike, are like the birds.

You're wrong there, he would say cutting me short.

We are like the birds who sing as if they have something urgent they need to say.

Come on, he would say. Speak for yourself. I have these conversations to humor you. It's you who has something urgent to say, not me. I'm just here to humor you.

66

• • • •

Mike do you hear that bird? I would ask him.

Which bird?

That incredibly melodious songbird that sings as if its life depended on it. The bird that sings as if it has something mysterious and urgent it desperately needs to say.

You mean that cardinal piping from the treetop over there, he would say, squinting looking off into the distance and spotting in the darkness of the forest the movement of a tiny bit of red no larger nor more visible in the thicket of trees than the red of a match head. It was incredible how sharp his senses were and I'd tell him.

Your senses are incredibly attuned.

So what, he would say. It's not as though I wanted to be here. It's not as though this is my chosen métier. Instead, I've been forced here against my will, and my senses have grown attuned as a result. It's a matter of survival.

Do you think, he would ask me in all seriousness, I would have been able to persist in this god-awful and hellacious place without having adapted to it in some way or another? It's regretful that I have this—these sharpened senses—to show for it.

You see these woods?

Which woods?

These woods. These woods here.

Oh yeah, he would say. I've been here so long I've forgotten to take notice. It's my way of surviving, no doubt. Without these methods of survival, I would have perished years ago. Instead, I carry on.

We carry on because we have no choice.

It's our instinct to carry on, he would say. Without this instinct to persist, which is the most powerful instinct I have ever experienced, I would have gladly perished years ago. In fact I wish I could die but I don't have the courage, which is just another way of saying, it's my instinct to persist.

As it is mine, I would say feeling particularly bleak in my heart's core. Instead I carry on.

Yes. It is our curse.

* * * *

So that day out in the woods listening to the incredibly beautiful voice of the cardinal I would ask him if he could see it.

Do you see the bird making that beautiful song as if it has something mysterious and urgent it must say?

Yes, over there, he would say looking in the direction of the bird. It's a cardinal.

You identify the red head of that cardinal as if you were in a white room and on the opposing wall was a splotch of vivid red paint. Instead we are peering off into an incredibly dense thicket and you see in the maze of trees and branches the red tip of that bird's head as if it were as easy as seeing a blotch of red paint in a white room.

I wish I were in a white room, he would say. Surrounded by four walls. This would be paradise for me. What I used to take for granted, the four walls of my home, I now long for with an urgency I can barely contain.

You see that bird over there piping? I would ask.

Of course, I see it, he'd say without even squinting in the direction of the bird in question. Do you see it? he'd ask.

Yes there it is, I would say staring off into the same direction trying to locate the bird by sound. Positioning my head both vertically and horizontally according to the direction from which the birdsong came I would position my head just so and stare off in that direction as if I were peering down a long tube and there at the end of the tube was the little red head of a matchstick that was really just a cardinal camouflaged except for its head in the deep green night of the thick forest canopy.

You see that bird over there . . .

It would hold still for a second clinging to a branch making its song and we would both watch and listen to its intensely beautiful voice say its urgent and mysterious thing for all and none to hear.

What do you think it's saying? I would ask him.

Nonsense, probably. Probably nothing. It's just the call of a cardinal. You've heard one you've heard them all.

It's like the most beautiful aria don't you think?

No. I don't think so. It's only a reflex it has. To pipe and sing. Same as my reflex, which is a reflex to want to escape this place so desperately I cannot even put it into words.

To have something on your heart and sing like that. It must be wonderful. Reminds me of you and me, I would say.

How so?

How we like to talk so much.

You like to talk. Not me. I'm here only to humor you. I'm here because I have no choice but to be here. If I were here of my own accord I would talk—enjoy talking to you—but the fact that I'm here by force and wish to be any other place than this place keeps me from feeling as though this conversation we have going on here is just a pleasant little conversation. What it really is is just two people flapping their jaws making noise.

69

But of course it's conversation.

It's no more conversation than the noise that bird makes is song. You and I talk no more than that bird sings. But birds don't sing. They make noise. Only humans sing. Humans who aren't bound in a wilderness against their will sing, but those who are bound in a wilderness against their will—poor unfortunates such as you and I—merely make noise like that bird in the distant tree, for don't you see, he would say to me in all reasonableness, to be bound in a wilderness against your will is the most inhuman—the most dehumanizing fate imaginable.

We may be here because we have no choice but that doesn't mean we can't sing.

We can attempt to sing but what we sing isn't song it's noise, just as this so-called conversation isn't conversation, but noise.

You may consider it noise but I consider it what it is our conversation is our freedom song just as that bird's terribly urgent music is its freedom song.

And unlike that bird that can fly out of these woods willy-nilly as it pleases we are stuck in these godforsaken woods hoping against hope to one day escape it only the longer I stay locked up in these woods the more I realize that there's nothing more poisonous than to long to leave this place.

We're here because we have no choice, I would correct.

Yes. This is true. I'm glad you're beginning to see the truth of your situation.

The truth of my situation, I would tell him, is that I have a premonition that one day or another when I least expect it some-one will arrive from out of nowhere and take me away from here.

That's the truth of your situation, he would say. But your sit-uation isn't true. You sit here locked in these woods thinking you'll one day get out of here, which is true. But that you'll one day get out of here, leaving these woods behind is the falsest illusion you could possibly maintain.

To live in these woods and think there is no escape whatsoever is even worse don't you think?

No. I don't think.

Seriously.

Look, he would say: you believe there's nothing worse than the truth, which is obvious from your actions. Whereas I believe there is nothing better than the truth no matter how bitter or sorrowful that truth may be. Listen, he would say to me in the most sagacious way imaginable, trust me on this. The truth is the best medicine for someone stuck in such a god-awful situation as you or I.

You see that bird, I would say.

Yes. Of course I see it, he would say without turning his head.

Reminds me of you and me the way it sings. You and I are very like that bird.

Ridiculous, he would say to me tugging at his beard looking over his shoulder that nervous tic.

Not ridiculous.

Yes ridiculous, he'd say. That bird flew into these woods and it will fly out of these woods when it so desires. You and I, on the other hand, were cast into these woods against our will, and no matter how much we will it, we will never escape. Don't you see that bird mocks us with its song? If you want to know what that bird is saying, it's laughing at us is what. It thinks we are the silliest people imaginable because we are as unable as it is able to leave these woods at the drop of a leaf. No matter how much you or I desire it, we are no more like that bird than his song is an aria. Birds pipe. Caruso sings!

• • • •

It was amazing how beautiful the birds could be arriving like a beneficence to all those stranded out here in the wilderness against their own will—stranded because they had been rebuked for no other reason than they were being exactly who they were designed to be nothing more nor less. To be who you were: this became the explanation that one carried around in one's heart while stranded out here in this godforsaken wilderness—to be who you were nothing more nor less was the reason for the rebukement we often thought to ourselves but there could have been countless reasons some logical some not so logical. Perhaps we were purged from the world and discharged into these forest preserves because we had been the opposite of lucky. A lucky person is in the right place at the right time but we happened to be the inverse: at the wrong place on the right time when the world was doing its purging. Perhaps we were purged only because the sky happened to be blue or cloudy or partly cloudy and the temperature was 57 degrees Fahrenheit or because we happened to have two quarters minted in 1975 jangling in our pockets or because we were ideological vegans in a meat-eating universe. Who can say why we were rebuked? No one who was sent out into this wilderness was ever told the cause of the rebukement. The rebukement just came out of the blue like a winter storm: fierce, unrelenting, pitiless. It was pitiless to be stuck in such a place no way out. How many hours—countless no doubt—have I spent in this hovel pondering my fate? Sometimes I would lie awake at night and ask, why me, and the woods seemed to answer nothing personal your name just happened to come up.

How long had I lain in my hovel feeling worn down by my fate—worn down so as I could barely move as if the weights of gravity had changed by several factors and were pulling me down so I could barely move—I am here, I tell myself sitting alone in my hovel no escape, for being exactly who I am nothing more nor less and sometimes it was the case that whenever I was feeling alone in my heart's core and lost so I didn't know how to proceed I would train myself to listen to the birdsong that was always readily available: it was best to listen to the birds in the early morning just before dawn and second best to listen to them in the evening as the sun set. During the day you heard mostly crows and sparrows and cardinals and grackles but during the early morning you heard the most melodious songbirds imaginable. Often, I would sit in my little hovel clipping my nails as the sun arose, and I would tell myself to listen to the birds piping outside. There is no more beautiful music, I would tell myself, than the singing of these lovely songbirds that have traveled during the night to avoid hawks and other predatory birds—traveled the night to sit on a branch outside my hovel and console me. It was as if the songbirds that had flown through the night had alighted upon the branches outside my hovel to humor me with the beauty of their song and I would tell Mike whenever I saw him particularly after a morning listening to the chorus of a beautiful flock of songsters how lucky we were.

We're lucky, I would tell Mike running into him on the trail. Some wake up listening to the radio or to their TVs but we wake up with this: the chirping of birds. Is there any music more beautiful than this?

73

It's not music, he'd point out. It's just a bunch of birds making nonsense sounds.

It's music, I would argue. You can chart what they say with notes if you knew how to write music: this one sings in F sharp, this one in A minor. It's very obvious there is order and melody to this birdsong and therefore it's obvious that they're making music. I only wish I knew what compelled them to sing.

Sex, of course, Mike would say. It's the only thing that moves any of us to song.

Or the joy of it, I would point out. For certainly there must be a joy associated with making such beautiful music.

Yes, they're happy they can fly out of this wilderness just as easily as they flew into it. They're happy because they can be in Florida by tomorrow morning if they so desire. Whereas you and I are stuck the rest of our days out in this terrible wilderness no getting out it makes me sick.

Just then he'd tug at his beard look over his shoulder to see if any person or malevolent being were coming after him and not certain whether someone was or not he took off into the dark and thorny brambles as if being chased by the devil himself and I could tell by the way he went whether to follow or not—or to turn around and go a different way and so off I'd go in my own direction not knowing exactly where I was going but going off as if I had the most important business to attend to in the next five minutes.

Until—I would shout after him and then he in his incredibly melodious voice would shout back after me. Until Joseph. And off we were gone, gone like the wind as if like the wind there were some errand we desperately needed to attend to, but there never was an errand either for us or for the wind.

• • • •

We move like the wind, I would tell Mike from time to time whenever we passed each other running through the woods.

The wind is like the birds, Mike would point out. The wind too can escape these woods. While we, unlike the wind or your sing-song birds are stuck here.

But like the wind, I would point out, we move as if we have some destination we desperately need to get to.

The only destination I need to get to is out of these woods, but that has already been proven to me to be impossible.

There is no proof you'll never get out of here.

The proof I'll never get out of here is the fact that I'm still here after nine years fervently trying to get out of this god-damned place.

But your luck can change. Who knows in a moment's time anything can happen. What seemed perdurable and inescapable—these footpaths leading through the woods in an endlessly circuitous fashion—suddenly may lead somewhere.

Why are you always trying to make me laugh? Do I seem so glum to you?

I'm not trying to make you laugh I'm only trying to tell you that nine years is not a long enough time to come to the conclusion that you'll never escape these woods.

The fact is, Joseph, he would say, I can't go on another day thinking that just around the bend is an opening back into the world. I have to prepare for reality and the reality we both must prepare for—that is, if you are willing to face the world as it is and not as you want it to be—is that we are here for life, no escape, and these footpaths we wander are indeed circuitous, but follow them as we will, we must remember, they will never lead anywhere other than this exact spot—that is where we always seem to be meeting each other.

• • • •

And he had a point.

You have a point.

Of course, I have a point. I have been here longer than you and I know whereof I speak. What's more I'm not afraid to confront the truth of our situation.

Like you, I would tell him in an attempt to be solicitous of his point of view, I have noticed that instead of being straight paths leading through the brush and brambles of these woods, that our paths invariably bend in long slow arcs.

Yes. That's how they bend.

And yet when you run along these footpaths they invariably seem straight as pointing to some spot out of these woods.

And yet, he would say, they never lead out of the woods, do they?

Oh I'm sure though there must be one or another of these paths that leads out of the woods. We just have to find it is the problem.

And while we try finding it we merely move in slow circles around and around and around chasing our tails or as if caught in some maze that exceeds our ability to transcend it.

• • • •

Other times we would be passing along the footpaths that wound themselves through these woods and there Mike would be running toward me with alarming velocity and I would realize

76

going in his opposite direction that I too was moving with alarming velocity and it was the case that everybody else moved with alarming velocity through these woods as well as if there were something about the white-tailed deer that leapt and bounded through the woods that we perforce of our time spent locked up in these woods necessarily emulated. We were all swift of foot and agile, indeed all the time we spent in these woods made us so. And those who were newly rebuked by the world were often astonished by the speed with which we moved in these woods but it wasn't long before they too adopted the ways of everyone else including the animals and particularly the white-tailed deer in these woods. More often than not whenever one encountered another of us trapped in these woods that person too was moving with alarming velocity—and so the hand up in the air, hi hi, as we passed like two ships moving at incredible velocity through the night.

We moved with enormous velocity because what other choice was there? To amble about aimlessly without point or destination as if you didn't have a care in the world? And though we didn't have any cares to speak of other than the demands that living alone out here in the woods placed upon us, we nevertheless moved as if the world itself waited for our next step with bated breath. Oh how silly to write this now. How silly to record how seriously we placed each and every step we ever took in the wilderness.

* * * *

One can never be too careful.
No—one can't, he would say to me.
Each day living in this wilderness is incredibly difficult.

Yes it is, but we don't have any choice to speak of but endure the difficulty. Even if we choose not to endure the difficulty, the difficulty nevertheless remains and therefore we must endure it whether we care to or not.

What are you saying?

I'm saying we can endure the difficulty without even trying to endure the difficulty, because whether we choose to endure it or not is a matter of indifference; and yet even if we take choice out of it and face this difficulty with indifference, the difficulty itself remains, and it remains painful, inescapable, and profoundly oppressive.

I agree with you, I would say taking enormous succor from the wisdom of my friend and then as if I had triggered some great pain within him, up with the hand and then the other and before I knew it he was howling with a pain that was so real and agonizing I realized that the howl itself really wasn't a howl but carnal pain of a tortured man made audible. And it was the saddest most heartbreaking thing in the world to hear such a cry especially from such a noble man and yet before I could say so he turned and off he loped like a wolf even though neither he nor his howl were wolf-like. Instead he was the most sagacious man I have ever encountered and in a former life he had been a tax collector. But in this life in the woods he was tortured to the point of screaming.

• • • •

We stand here again.

Yes.

If only we were wolves I said to him apropos of nothing.

78

There were songbirds twittering in the dark green night of the forest and we were standing at a crossroads in the woods which weren't crossroads at all but our worn-down footpaths that had been established by the deer themselves but which we in our endless perambulations around and around had worn smooth and clean.

If only we were wolves, I said.

There had been a distant howl and I had made the observation that the howls of the men locked up in these woods often seemed like the howls of wolves themselves when he contradicted me and said,

But we aren't wolves.

And yet the howls sound remarkably like the howls of wolves don't you think?

But they are not the howls of wolves. You see. There you go again. If you just thought that they were the howls of men, which is what they are, you would be okay. But you can't just think the howls of men are the howls of men, you're always trying to compare them to something they're not. To you, the howls of the men are really just the howls of wolves. Just like these woods. You can't stop living with the delusion that you'll one day get out of here even though you won't.

I will. It's not a delusion. What's more I'll never escape believing I'll never escape.

It's a delusion like everything else in that brain of yours is a delusion.

If only we were wolves.

But we are not. We are men, he pointed out.

Yes, we are men and that is our curse perhaps: because we are men we long to leave these woods but had we been born

79

wolves these woods would be our home sweet home and never
would we have to contend with a desire to leave these woods.
Don't you see what I am saying? It would be a blessing to be a
wolf stuck in these woods. This would be the most wonderful
place imaginable but because we're men we have no choice but to
desire to leave this place.

What you're saying is—our desire to leave this place is no
different from the desire of the wolf to remain in this place.

Yes, to leave. To stay. What is different is the feral urge: one
to leave, one to stay. Had we only been bred with the feral urge
to stay none of this would be problematic.

But we were bred with the urges we have as the wolf was
bred with his urges and so we are separate, not the same.

Yet we must learn to think like wolves. Don't you see?

No. I don't.

What if, I would ask him, what if we thought like wolves
and felt comfortable here in these woods as if it were home
sweet home but nevertheless retained a curiosity about the world
outside of these woods. Might not the proverbial cat be skinned
under such conditions?

What if? What if? What if? There are so many what ifs with
you. It shows you have much to learn.

He was always so sagacious. So fucking relentlessly truthful
and I loved him for it and so I said in the most loving way imaginable: And what might that be?

That there are no what-ifs. That to think in what-ifs is
already to get lost on the road to delusion, no way out or back
home to the real.

But what if it were only a manner of speaking so to speak in
order to understand the world as it is?

80

There is no other way but to let that stuff go. What if I were still a tax collector on the outside world? Hmm? What if I were still shod in wingtip shoes and a blue pin-striped suit? What if I were such a man busy with his nine-to-five job and living in a home instead of these woods? What if I were able to visit these woods like everyone else visits these woods . . . come and go as I like? What if I ate custard pie and drank coffee with one creamer and two sugars and tipped the waitress fifteen percent, then left the diner to go about my business knocking on the doors of tax scofflaws? What if all of this were the case as it had once been the case before the world rebuked me; but, in addition, what if while being the case, the world, unlike what it did to me—rebuked me—this time rebuked someone else other than me or better yet left all the tax collectors and everyone else whom the world chose to rebuke to carry on with their day-to-day existence? What if? Don't you see? The what-ifs can carry on endlessly until we're back where we started, only to discover we'll never escape the reality of our situation so what's the point? Do you realize that if this were the world—all these what-ifs that I just conjured—then the world that you and I are now forced to occupy would be only the local forest preserves and, as such, would hardly register on our consciousness if they registered on it at all. And if that were the case, then the howls, if we heard them at all in these woods, would most likely be nothing more than the howls of wolves or more likely the coyote that we would hear while walking our dog by the leash; and we'd wonder at the novelty of that. We'd wonder at the sweet novelty of wild howling animals locked up in the local forest preserves, howling for all they were worth. Then our own dogs would take a shit, and we'd pick the shit up with plastic baggies over our hands, and we'd deposit the shit in a garbage can; then we'd return to our homes and forget we had ever heard the howling or thought about it. As it is, the world rebuked us into this nasty bit of foul and neglected forest; and when I can no longer take the pain of having been cast out here because of the unbearable condition of my situation, then I howl because I can't help it. I howl not like a wolf, but like a man, and it gives me no pride or satisfaction to realize that this is what I've been reduced to: a howling man grieving in pain because, though circumstances might have been different, yet in point of fact they aren't different than what they are; nor will they ever be different. And so, I howl. You can make fun of me if you please or you can think of me as some interesting curiosity related only by thought to the howling wolves in the local forest preserves, but there is nothing funny about my situation, nor about yours for that matter; and one day, I promise you, when you come to understand the truth of your situation—that these woods are your enemy and that you will never escape this place—then you too will find an inability to hold back from howling like a wild animal grieving in pain. It will seize you so that you won't know what's become of you; and then you won't be you any more, for you will have become only an urge to howl and rid yourself of the excess pain you can no longer contain. And, in truth, I admire you because this awful fate hasn't yet befallen you, but at the same time I am already sad beyond belief that, as surely as I stand here before you, so too do I know that this awful curse of howling will overtake you.

Nonsense, I would say. I love these woods too much for such a thing to happen.

Then there was the tug of the beard and the nervous tic: perhaps the beard tug and the nervous tic were methods he had concocted to ward off the emergence of a howl or perhaps it

82

was only what it was—a nervous tic and a tug of the beard—but a moment later he was off running on his circuitous route through the woods and not long thereafter I was off running on mine.

Until, Joseph.

And then over my shoulder: Until.

● ● ● ●

In the sunlight radiant from shafts of light standing there in his magnificent beard he was standing before me as if anticipating my arrival and I came upon him as I ran leaping and dodging through the woods moving faster through the woods than I had ever moved before. When I came to rest I smiled at him and perhaps because I was filled with an inexplicable love for this hateful place I told him a truth I knew he didn't want to hear but that since we were going to be truthful I decided to tell him anyway.

I have a truth for you.

For me? From you? What a gift! Why now?

Because I realize how we are different.

You're only realizing now?

We are different, I told him in all solicitude, because unlike you who longs to get out of these woods even though you know you won't which in turn invariably triggers one of your howls, I have learned to love these woods and because I love the beauty of these woods as a wolf might love them which is to say as if they are the most important friend in the world I have ever known then I have found comfort and sanctuary here and so I know as a matter of fact that unlike you, I will never find myself possessed of the howling curse that seems to grip you and so many others stranded in this wilderness. I know I shall never yell.

83

When you arrive at the truth, as you no doubt one day
shall, about your situation, which is the saddest story known to
man—that you will never escape these woods that you have been
rebuked by the world and cast into, then you will howl. Trust me.
Telling you this gives me no pleasure. That you still love these
woods and believe someone will one day take you out of here
also gives me a bit of pleasure; but since this will never happen
. . . since this illusion that you live with—that you will escape this
place—will never happen, then you will, upon realizing this, find
some tree to climb up into and from the top of the tree you will
howl like a monkey, not because you are a monkey but because
the pain of your situation is so unbearable there is no other
adequate response to it other than to climb a tree and howl like
a monkey even though, believe you me, you aren't a monkey
but a human. You will climb a tree and howl like a human howls,
for there is no escape other than through a howl of the terrible
truths that will invariably confront you when you are ready, either
by design or by force of will, to hear and understand these terrible truths.

Of course, I pointed out, there is death. Death is always an
escape.

Death would be an escape if we had the courage to exit on
our own time and by our own hand, but I don't have the will for
that.

Neither do I.

And so we persist. What other choice is there?

That's what I want to know.

Persist, whether difficult or not: whether standing at the
crossroads as we stand right now or buried as if already dead in
the hovels we have constructed for escape into sleep.

84

* * * *

Other times when he seemed truly desperate nine years in no escape and ready to howl he pointed out a different truth:

We can always kill ourselves and be done with it.

Of course, we won't do that.

Of course, we will. That is, if your proverbial cat suddenly needed skinning.

If my proverbial cat needed skinning then we would learn to think like a wolf while remaining a man.

Unless we kill ourselves, which I would happily do were it not for this instinct to persevere.

* * * *

Do you know, I remember once telling Mike, make no mistake: you and I may yet live to a ripe old age.

Yes, our life term has likely been greatly abridged, and I would shorten it more with my own hand were it not for this instinct to persist.

I love these woods as if they are my dearest friend, but if I could live to a ripe old age I would be grateful for that as well.

Not me.

Grateful for a long life the way I'm grateful for these woods.

Which woods? he'd ask me.

Why these woods here.

Oh. I'm sorry you mentioned it. I try so very hard to forget them but you're always bringing them up.

Sorry I would say. But I do love them I can't help it.

You're fooling yourself.

85

Nonsense. I love sitting up in the branches feeling the tree
sway beneath me and looking up through the tangle at the sky: at
night I can make out the stars like sitting in the crow's nest.

Yes. Literally, like sitting in a crow's nest. And what a shame
that is, he would say. Never thought I'd be talking to a guy who
literally sat in a crow's nest day after day, no end in sight.

It isn't so bad, I would tell him.

What isn't?

These woods . . . When the weather is nice it's quite doable.

If it were doable, I would not want to escape it with a wish
so fervent I do not even know how to express it. If it were doable,
I would be a visitor to these woods, but I am not a visitor. I was
cast into these woods because of an inexplicable rebukement,
which, though I try to fathom the cause, yet the cause escapes
me; and, though I fathom an escape, the means of escaping
eludes me. If I could sit in a crow's nest like you appear to be able
to do and dwell in that bird's nest as a bird dwells in it, with no
thought whatsoever of escaping at the dropping of a leaf just
merely by taking wing, then like you, I might say, these woods on
a peaceful day are quite doable; but since I have been purged by
the world into this dark place, I cannot think that even a moment
here is doable because I never wanted to be here in the first
place. If I were to think that any moment here were doable—as
you appear able to do in your crow's nest—then I might fall into
the trap of accommodating myself to the idea of dwelling here
indefinitely; and if I were to accommodate myself to such an idea,
then I too would also wish, like you, for a long life. But if I did all
this, then I would lose all hope of ever actually making good on
my singular desire to leave this place. As it is, if I died today, I'd
be happy. But happier still if the dying, my dying, had already hap-

86

pened rather than leaving me here all alone in these inescapable woods wondering how on earth I'm going to escape them.

But to live to a ripe old age, I would say egging him on. At least you would have that to hold up to the rebuking world.

It's not something I hold, this instinct to persist; and if I held it, I would happily let it go, but I can't. As to living to a ripe old age, I can think of no greater hell than to do so, particularly if the condition for living to a ripe old age meant I were to live burdened by the ridiculous hope of wanting to escape these woods, even while knowing that there was never a vainer thought that one rebuked into this crust of wilderness could entertain. As a result, I sometimes, even now, dwell on the idea of not living to a ripe old age but of committing myself, like a dead skunk fallen in the high grass, to an ignominious end. To fall where I fall and to let happen after that what may happen. To waste away as flesh and bones, then as bones, then as the slow naught of my ever disappearance. Only right now I don't have the courage to do myself in, and I don't want to die like a common skunk.

• • • •

Other times he would say to me this: if I had the heart to do myself in, then I would do myself in. Had it already happened, I would not have to dwell on it's happening, and there would be peace in that. As it is, for now, I don't have the heart to do myself in.

That is because you hope to escape these woods, I would say.

Yes, exactly. I hope to escape these woods so I live on another day, even though to live on another day is often the most

87

difficult thing in the world to accomplish, regardless of whether one wants to accomplish it or not. There is also the fact that I don't want to die untended and alone like the common skunk, even though—even now—the idea of dying like a common skunk seems the most realistic way of all to escape this place.

But there is dignity in a skunk as there is a dignity in all living things that come to rest and die.

Skunks don't think about dignity, he would point out with beautiful sagacity. Only humans think about dignity. If I were a skunk, I wouldn't think about dignity, and so I wouldn't mind getting struck down where I stand and moldering in the high grass. Yet I'm a human, and as such I am cursed to possess notions of dignity; and, at the very least, these notions of dignity hold me back from that second form of escape—which, if I can't escape by leaving these woods, I might escape, as you suggest, by some form of immolation or other.

＊ ＊ ＊ ＊

Regarding that other, I would ask him: what other ways are there?

In a place like this I can think of countless, he would say. And he'd say it as if the question itself were something to savor but really there was nothing at all to savor about this business and he let me know as much when he frowned a moment later to tell me so.

Well, there is death by illness, he would say. Then death by neglect, then death by tree-limb falling struck down in storm; there is getting struck down in storm by lightning and falling to die where one is felled. There is death by snakebite, and death by spider; there is death by disease or by insect or by parasite, and there is death by hunger and by thirst. There is death by injury and death by age. There is death by heart attack and death by fever. There is death by violence perpetrated by one of the armed maniacs living in this godforsaken place, and there is death by bleeding. There is death by falling, and death by freezing. There is death by self-inflicted gunshot wound, and death by drowning. I could go on. I've seen it all, my nine years out here. And don't forget, of course, the worst way of death possible: death by merely giving up and failing after too many days to leave one's shelter. Of death by shelter. Of death by failing to escape. Of death by death. And then there is your idea. Death by immolation, by burning or getting burnt: a great conflagration might one day overtake this place, and that may be how both you and I eventually end up escaping these woods. However, even though no one else cares what becomes of me, whether I leave these fucking woods or not, whether I die today or live another, I care. It means something to me. It's a goal of mine to survive.

It's our instinct.

Yes, he'd say. You're very right about that, Joseph. Then tug at his beard and off he'd go running through the trees and brambles at an unbelievable speed and off I'd go following him in my own way running as fast as I could along the footpaths that though they looked straight invariably bent and blocked any exit from these godforsaken woods.

* * * *

Other times we'd be swimming in the muddy river among the lilies and reeds and long river grasses. We'd strip naked and plunge into the water in the heat and he'd emerge from the depths looking like Poseidon his huge mane of uncut hair and that magnificent beard of his. And we'd spend whole afternoons wading in the water during the heat, the flies and mosquitoes would gather in clouds around our heads and we'd dive down and swim upstream against the current or we'd turn around and swim with the current and in the flood pools and lost bays of the eddying river we'd swim among whole schools of carp and bullheads we'd feel them swim among our legs and the smell of the muddy river would be strong in our noses and it was at such times I'd be filled with such a love for the woods that I wouldn't be able to contain myself and I'd say to him,

I love this place.

Which place? he'd ask.

This. Right here. This place. I feel the luckiest man on earth to occupy this place right now. And he'd try to snap me out of it.

Snap out of it, he'd say.

Snap out of what?

Get over this infatuation you have for this place.

It isn't infatuation, I'd tell him. It's true love.

Part 3
Death
in the Woods,
High Up
in the Trees

The river was a thing to reckon with. It had a smell which you never forgot if you smelled it only for a brief period of time but if you lived near the river you grew so accustomed to it that you forgot the smell of the river. In the spring the mud banks would be crawling with snakes and green frogs that we'd snare and we'd take the legs unskinned and cook them over hot coals and it's one of the foods as well as wild raspberries and strawberries that got us through the spring and summer. The rain would fall for days and sometimes I would stand in the shelter of trees watching it fall into the river and I would think of lines I used to know before I was rebuked into this wilderness, lines about the rain. Even a fool knows how to get out of the rain. But not I—I now thought—stranded in this wilderness. It took an enormous amount of forbearance and training to get used to the rain the wet the mud and when one could take it no longer there was always the option of becoming one with the water. Of walking into it in the storm wading deep into the river feeling the current push against you half hoping to be washed away but knowing all these many months living alone untended in the woods has made you too strong and savvy to drown so easily.

Yes the water, I would tell Mike submerged up to my chin—a virtual mud-man submerged one with the earth. Yes the water. There is always water to wash all that ails you away!

He would suck water into his mouth and like a great fountain his cheeks puffed out he would spit it out to me and that is all he would say on the subject.

• • • •

Other times we'd be gathered around a small fire and our
fires in the woods were always small discreet fires and we seldom
had fires but if we did have a fire then our fire was incredibly
small and discreet and we huddled close to the fire but not so
close we singed our fingers but close enough so we could receive
the maximum amount of heat our fire had to give and it was
something you learned living so long in the woods, how to lean
near a discreet fire and make the most of it, and our tiny discreet
fire would burn on through the night and he and I would be leaning over the fire our teeth chattering and there was nothing said
between us for hours at a time for what was there either he could
tell me or vice versa that we didn't already deeply know.

I can sit across this fire from you and say nothing and yet it's
like we're communicating on the deepest level imaginable.

What did you say? I would say out loud for he sometimes
tried to communicate things to me through his eyes and I didn't
always understand what those things were.

Your eyes, I would say. They're trying to tell me something.

If you didn't understand then forget it, he would say. After
all, we're not husband and wife. No reason to pretend you can
know what I'm thinking without my having to say it.

That's not to say, I would say in all solicitude, that's not to
say you wouldn't be a good husband for you have the greatest
heart of anyone I have ever known.

Tell my wife that, he would say.

Tell your wife . . . you don't have a wife.

I don't? How would you know? Then there's but the tug at
his beard the look over his shoulder and off he'd go running off in

the woods on the darkest and coldest of nights imaginable and I would lean near the fire my teeth chattering and I wouldn't dare fall asleep until the last ember had expired.

* * * *

Tell me, I once asked him. Have you ever been married?
Never.
Then what was that you said back there about your wife?
I said nothing of the sort. You must have imagined it.
Or maybe I saw something of the sort in your eyes.

* * * *

Other times we would lean near the fire our teeth chattering and from the darkness the priest would emerge and without saying a word he'd join our company. He'd sit down as close to the discreet fire as possible without singeing his fingers and it was a sign, a sad sign no doubt, that he too—like both Mike and me—had been in these woods too long. He too—like Mike and me—knew only too well about the discreet fires one must set if one is to have fires and remain in these woods undiscovered.

Hi, he would say, without saying it and we would hear him talking to himself for he often talked to himself without saying a word.

Father forgive me for I have sinned, he would say mumbling to himself and it wasn't very long being with the priest when you realized he was a different sort altogether. He seemed hardly to care what misfortune befell him out in the wilderness. He viewed his misfortune as a penance of sorts: if Jesus could gnash and

95

cry in the garden of Gethsemane then so could he. If John the
Baptist could wander in the wilderness starving on a diet of bugs
while he waited for his savior to come then so could he. What's
more the priest was extremely guilt ridden always apologizing
for something or another he had done in his life before he'd
been rebuked by the world and cast out here to persist as long
as he could persist or perish and occasionally yes one or another
of us perished out here and if you did perish out here alone in
the woods you perished of natural causes dropping off in the
quietest way imaginable as if for a nap never to open your eyes
again—or else you were killed by knife or gun or strangling as the
case may be and then left to rot. If you did drop off it was likely
you stayed dead at the spot you had died in until someone or
another sensing either your absence from the various hunts or
gatherings we would periodically have or another person smelling
your moldering corpse would come and discover you leaning up
against the tree in the exact same position you had died the flesh
already decayed on your skull and bones and the flies buzzing
around you and the stink. Then there would be the decision what
to do with your body and it was one of the unspoken rules that
continued to be ratified with each burial that if we did find a
fallen body, if one of our own brethren who had been rebuked
by the world had dropped dead and was discovered moldering in
the high grass so to speak, then we would perform the simplest
burial imaginable burying our fallen brother here in the wilderness
to which he had been discharged. We would be notified of the
deceased by a messenger who was extraordinarily fleet of foot
whom everyone called the Grim Reaper though his actual name
was Bob. He was also known as Blind-eyed Bob when he wasn't

sending out messages about the dead for he had a twitch in his left eye. It was Bob's job when someone died to be the messenger because he was so fleet of foot and also because he was so beautifully nimble afoot and in spirit and if he announced your death he announced it in the most succinct way imaginable. His obituary for the deceased was always the same. He would arrive from nowhere finding you with extreme precision wherever it was you were sitting or standing and he would merely say: And so it's happened.

It was a code word, really, and so it's happened, but we all knew what it meant. It meant that another person stranded in these woods unable to escape had in his way escaped in the most miserable way imaginable by dropping down dead of natural or unnatural causes.

And so it's happened, you would say in disbelief worried that next time the same words might be applied to you. Who was it this time? you would ask.

It was Mink, he might say, or Jefferson. Found him dead in a slough, buried by leaves, his flesh leached off his bones, half eaten by fox.

Will there be a burial?

This evening. Sundown.

I'll be there, you would say. Then a complicated thing would be done with our hands to indicate farewell and with that the messenger would be on his way moving along through the woods with incredible agility and grace running and dodging through the brush and trees at breakneck speed to spread the grim and unhappy news.

• • • •

The burial grounds were in a hidden place in the woods not locatable by anyone but the Grim Reaper and the Grim Reaper's Second: Wyatt, a tall lean fellow whom everyone just called Earp even though he wasn't Wyatt Earp, he was Wyatt Smith, and there were those who didn't even bother calling him Earp but quite simply Burp. And it was the Grim Reaper and Burp who were the keepers of the location of the burial grounds. And at first it had just been the Grim Reaper who knew the precise location of the burial ground but then after a spate of burials a general consensus arose that there ought to be someone other than Blind-eyed Bob who knew where the burial grounds were.

For what if he should go blind in his other eye? someone or another exclaimed to which Blind-eyed Bob had to point out, Look it's only a twitch in my left eye is all, and I can still see out both eyes. I am not blind, I'm only called blind, he would say, quite defensively.

Nevertheless, someone else might observe, what if you should go blind in both eyes Blind-eyed Bob? Then who would show us the way to the burial grounds where our brethren are buried?

Or . . . or . . . Hunter pointed out, What if Blind-eyed Bob should be stricken in the place that he is standing? What if Blind-eyed Bob should drop? Then who would notify us of Blind-eyed Bob's death and furthermore who would lead us to the burial grounds to bury Blind-eyed Bob with all the other brethren?

Certainly not me, Hunter would say. It's already bad enough I've got to lead you louts on all these hunts.

How nice it would be, someone else shouted loud enough

you wondered did he think us deaf or was it only the first time in a very long time he spoke and so he was unpracticed at how to modulate his volume. This one's name was Fred and he shouted, How nice it would be, Hunter, if we actually killed enough game on one of your so-called hunts to sustain us in our hours of need!

Well if you could keep up with me, Old Man, Hunter shouted (as if he too were deaf) out to Fred, who was no older than twenty-seven years, instead of always falling behind. If you could manage the flank-end of our hunt as you have been positioned to do so, perhaps fewer of the deer would escape around the perimeter of our attack and we might be more successful in our hunts!

Okay, I've heard enough—Adam, who was the leader of our group said for he was running out of patience. I think we need to appoint a Second to follow the Grim Reaper around. That-a-way, if anything happens to Blind-eyed Bob, we will still have someone to find Blind-eyed Bob where he drops and guide us to the burial grounds where we can lay him with our brethren.

But I have no intention, shouted Blind-eyed Bob, loud enough to startle even Fred.

You have no intention what? Adam asked, patiently.

Of dropping.

Okay, are there are any volunteers? Adam asked, changing the subject.

In fact no one wanted to volunteer for the job of being Blind-eyed Bob's Second. No one wanted to be Grim Reaper II. No one wanted to volunteer partly because keeping up with the fleet-footed Grim Reaper was such a challenge, partly because no one locked up in these woods wanted to know with any specificity where in the woods the burial grounds were kept. Even though we all knew exactly where the burial grounds were kept for how could you not know—it was too small a woods and we had spent too long a time wandering the woods not to know by name every tree, brush, and bramble in the godforsaken place but even though each and everyone of us knew exactly where in the woods the hidden location of the burial grounds was, even though each of us knew also that sooner or later we too were likely to end up buried in these burial grounds that is if we were lucky enough to have our bodies discovered where they had fallen by Blind-eyed Bob and now his Second, nevertheless none of us wanted to admit we knew where in the woods the burial grounds were. Nor did we want to confess to ourselves or to anyone else for that matter that it would be one of the luckier conditions of our exile out in these woods should we one day not only be struck down where we stand but should we be discovered fallen where we had dropped by Blind-eyed Bob and his Second so that proper burial rituals could be performed. So when Adam said, Are there any volunteers for a Second to the Grim Reaper? it wasn't a surprise to any of us that there were no volunteers for not only did we all want to pretend that the burial grounds did not exist but we also wanted to pretend, by extension, that we would not really need to know where the burial grounds existed because we wouldn't be one of those unfortunates who would end up buried in the burial ground because we, unlike they the fallen, weren't going to be so unlucky to die in these woods, on the contrary, we were one of the chosen few destined to escape this godforsaken place. Even though as Mike liked to point out, this truth, that we were going to escape, wasn't a truth but a lie that we needed to live with because the lie that we were going to escape made palatable the truth that we weren't going to escape and that as a result all our remaining time was going to be spent in the woods and that the

very best case scenario was in point of fact that we would drop
in the woods, be discovered, and the proper burial rituals would
be performed. So when it was asked, who was willing to volunteer to be Blind-eyed Bob's Second, it wasn't a surprise that no
one volunteered to be Blind-eyed Bob's Second because to do so
would mean essentially confessing the truth of your situation that
you were never going to escape these woods and there wasn't a
soul among us even though we knew the ultimate truth of that
truth who wanted to admit the truth of that truth and so we all
remained quiet and then straws were pulled and dice were tossed
and when these methods of random choice failed to produce
suitable results then we all gathered round Blind-eyed Bob. He
was blindfolded, spun around and around in a circle so he could
barely stand, and when he came to a stop he lifted up his hand
and pointed and he was so tipsy off balance that it couldn't be
decided whether Blind-eyed Bob was pointing at me or at Burp;
but a moment later Burp saved the day by stepping forward and
that's how Burp became the Grim Reaper's Second.

And so at sundown we would all loosely congregate at the
limestone park building that was near the terminus point of the
forest preserve road and in view of Dam No. 2—the small dam that
blocked up the Des Plaines river. We gathered, the whole tribe of
us at sundown regardless of who else—what tourists from town
might be picnicking or hiking in the woods. And up and down the
forest preserve roads you saw the station wagons, the pickup
trucks and minivans, the domestic sedans and motorcycles—mostly
Harley-Davidson but there were Hondas and Kawasakis as well,
but up and down the forest preserve road on any given day there
were all these sorts of vehicles and people here for a variety of
reasons: to pick up drugs, to pick up prostitutes (hetero- and

101

homosexual), to walk the dogs (mostly golden retrievers and labs) or quite simply to walk arm and arm through the woods admiring the beauty of the place, and we couldn't gather, the whole tribe of us, in view of all these visitors without doing a little preening and peacocking for each of us secretly hoped that someone or another, that one of them coming into the woods was doing so for the express purpose of claiming one of us to take us out of here and thereby end our penance of forty days out in the wilderness though for some of us it was considerably and mind-bogglingly longer than anything like the so-called forty days which in retrospect would have been a blessing indeed.

Oh how we liked to preen and peacock for the visitors. How we liked to show off who we were. Mike's beard, for instance, was always well groomed on these occasions though I must confess that I always made sure that I was well shaved and that my hair was combed and that the clothes I was wearing were reasonably clean.

● ● ● ●

At least we have the priest, I would say when Mike got ruminating on his own mortality.

Yes, we do have him.

And you know bodies are always being found in these woods so even if you were to drop dead like the common skunk and molder for several days as if you were no better than any of the other animals that have fallen dead to decay on the spot they have fallen nevertheless we will sooner or later discover your body.

And so you might say we have finally solved the skunk dilemma.

The skunk dilemma? he asked raising his eyebrows and giving a little laugh.

Yes. The problem that if you fall down and die like a skunk yet sooner or later we will find and bury you and at least by so doing confer the appropriate dignity that burial rites naturally confer.

• • • •

You know what the worst thing is, being stranded in these woods no escape from them except by death is? Mike would ask me from time to time as we ran into each other in the woods.

What's the worst thing?

Dying and decaying in the spot in which you had died. Dying as if you were no better than the common skunk.

Why should you think yourself better than the common skunk? I would ask in all seriousness.

You may not think me better than the common skunk, but I think myself better than the common skunk.

We are all mortal after all, I would say to him especially if we were standing over the carcass of some dead animal or another.

I'm afraid you're right about that, he would say, though you are wrong about so much else.

Dust to dust, ashes to ashes.

But you see, he would say lifting his head and gazing at me with his luminous eyes, tugging at his beard. Those words: dust to dust, those are burial words. A man deserves burial words. A common animal, such as a skunk, that has fallen in the high grass doesn't need burial words. But a man . . .

That's what we have the priest for, I would say.

103

You're right about that. At least we have the priest.

And now we have our ritual thus ending the skunk dilemma.

* * * *

Our burials were possible of course because we had the priest. How else would we bury anyone out here in this god-forsaken place which I had grown to love with an almost carnal desire. It was one of the few luxuries we had our priest.

It's a luxury to have him, I would say to Mike both of us bent toward the fire to warm ourselves from the terrors of the night.

If you say so, Mike would say. As for me, I can hardly stand him.

Without the priest, I would say, there would be no such thing as a proper burial in this place because he consecrates the whole thing. Without the priest we would truly be stuck in this wilderness no escape, but with the priest to perform a proper burial we at least have a chance to die with some sort of dignity.

Yes, Mike would say, twisting his beard hairs, I suppose you're right.

* * * *

Without the priest it might not have been so easy to perform a proper burial but with the priest it was eminently doable. What's more we all recognized this to be the case so on some deep level we were all grateful to the priest even though most of the time we paid him no attention whatsoever, and if we paid any attention to him at all it was invariably of the most abusive kind.

· · · ·

You could meet the priest in the middle of the woods and
say hello to him and without even pausing, the prayers, which
he had been speaking to himself, would be verbalized and he'd
direct them at you. You could meet the priest in the middle of the
woods and say hi and without even pausing from his daily prayers
he would say in lieu of hi: I am not deserving of your forgiveness
(meaning god's forgiveness) for always I would say back: Forgiveness for what father? You haven't wronged me? But I have, he
would say carrying on his conversation with god as if I were his
(god's) surrogate.

Hello Father, I would say meeting him in the middle of the
woods.

Forgive me, he would say addressing not me but god above
though he was talking and looking directly at me. Forgive me, he
would say, for I am among those who have sinned most dearly.
So please, in your infinite mercy and wisdom, you who knows
everything that ever is and was forgive me and forgive what is
in my heart for I am god created and so what is in my heart was
put there by you and if it pleases you not to forgive me then
I stand humbled and unforgiven. I huddle here in these woods
among your most worthless creatures. I am those most worthless
and humble penitents who have sinned against their own better
judgment. You gave me judgment, but you also gave me what was
in my heart. Forgive me for what is in my heart. Forgive me if that
which is in my heart is more potent than my judgment, which you
have also bequeathed to me in your divine wisdom . . .

On and on he went nodding near the fire and once or twice
his beard would catch on fire for he grew the beard of a prophet.

105

And we would laugh whenever his beard caught on fire and once or twice Adam, who was among all of us the most sociable person imaginable, would laugh after tenderly putting the priest's beard out and say, Behold the burning bush. His beard burns as if it's the burning bush!

Other times when Adam would run into the priest he would say, Priest, you need your beard burnt. It has grown too long. Burn it and see what commandments may descend from the mount.

There were other times too of course after the priest became famous for his burning beard when those who had never seen it on fire wished to see it on fire and they would taunt him with their lighters or with chunks of burning coals that they'd hold close to his beard. Some would subdue him and hold him and one person would cry out, Behold the burning beard! And another would say, Child molester! And yet others would say, He walks around here like some sort of prophet. Let's make a martyr of him. And one night they did make a martyr of him. Several held him while one or two secured him with a rope around his neck and just before they hung him they set his beard on fire—and the howls you heard coming from the good priest were the most terrible and horrible howls imaginable and while he hung there burning in the tree I couldn't help but remember how incredibly tender and gentle he was, always asking forgiveness for one such thing or another. And the way he counseled us by telling us it wasn't our fault we were rebuked and sent into this godforsaken wilderness. We were rebuked for no other reason than being exactly who we were. And something took hold of me that night: a terror to do anything whatsoever to save him. How could I save him? I asked myself that night watching him burn in the treetops.

How could I save him from his immolation out here in this god-forsaken wilderness and also hope to save myself? If I hoped to save myself I had to survive and if I wanted to survive there was no way I could help him burning up there all alone in the treetops. So they hung him by his neck, which I didn't believe was going to happen even as they strung the rope around his neck, then they set his beard on fire, which I also didn't think was going to happen and even as he was hanged there was a surreal and unbelievable quality to the whole thing. It seemed so extemporized. What had started out as a sort of joke escalated more quickly than I thought things like this could happen into a hanging and there I was standing at the outskirts of the crowd asking myself, should I go ahead and try to save him? But it was already too late. He was already beyond help burning and screaming up there in the treetops—his howl so very different from any of the howls I have ever heard issue from the heart of a man—and it was better that way, I thought. He has been sacrificed to his lord. It must be better that way for him. And who was I, I thought. Who the hell did I think I was to save him? I was a nobody after all and a nothing and the sooner I realized that the better off I was, stranded out in this godforsaken wilderness. The sooner I realized that I was nothing, the better off I was. If I pretended I was anything other than nothing then this being stranded in the woods would be the most difficult thing imaginable. And so in my infinite nothingness I stood on the outskirts of that mob while they hanged and burned the priest—and the shouts: Take that you goddamned child molester, a child of god well let god give you something you gave those little boys. But I get ahead of myself. That was a different night. Not the night the father came and sat with us. The father was always fond of Mike and me. You could tell he was fond of us. He never directly indicated that he liked us but if he caught us nodding by the fire he invariably sat with us. He sat very quietly in our circle and never interrupted what Mike and I had to say between ourselves. He just sat with us for company perhaps. For it was miserable and lonely out in the woods and one always desired company. But not everyone stranded and alone in this wilderness was worth keeping company with in fact the priest avoided everybody else in the woods and now you see it was for good reason and I try to remember where Mike was the night the priest got hanged. But I don't remember. Perhaps like me he was standing on the outskirts of the mob wondering if he should do something to save the priest or if it wouldn't be altogether better to just stand aside and watch. Let the mob have its day for if you ever try to interfere with a mob, you may one day rue that day. So up the priest went, by his neck, hanging by noose and rope. There was Hunter, he strung the cord around the Father's neck, and there was Adam directing the Grim Reaper or Blind-eyed Bob to pull the cord and others grabbed hold of the cord and yanked him up into the tree. And Adam, the great showman that he was, grabbed a burning stick from the fire and holding it close to the priest's beard, smiled at him. Forgive me, the priest said to Adam though he wasn't talking to Adam. Forgive me, the priest said as if in prayer to his god above though he spoke directly at Adam who held the burning stick near his beard. Forgive me, the priest said.

I forgive you, Adam said.

And someone else yelled out. For what? Forgive you for what? For child molestation? I was an altar boy, turn to me and ask me for forgiveness.

And another one shouting out, You weren't an altar boy.

The only time you've ever been inside a church is to rob from its coffers.

And the priest saying to himself and his god above, though he spoke to all of us: spoke to each of us as if he were addressing each one of us. I am sorry for what I have done. I am sorry for what is in my heart, but god-made that I am, you put what is in my heart there. You put judgment in my heart, and you put desire in my heart. And you knew even as you put it in my heart that my desire would overwhelm and overpower my judgment even though I had always wanted my judgment to prevail. Even though I have done everything I could to honor the judgment you have given me, I succumbed to my desire, which, it turned out was more than I could resist even though, even as you put both judgment and desire in my heart, you knew not only would the desire win out over my judgment, but that I would sacrifice my life to my judgment, and failing against my desire that I would spend the rest of my days in this miserable scrap of land called the forest preserves. You knew that I would be cast out here for being nothing more nor less than what I am and always have been. You knew I would be cast out here for expressing my essence in the world and that that essence, which was your essence, would cause all this to happen. And even so, I am sorry.

And with that Adam held the torch to the priest's beard setting it on fire and a writhing and screaming issued forth from the body of the priest as he was hoisted up by rope from his neck and left to burn in the treetops like an effigy. Only the priest wasn't an effigy but a writhing howling being burning on the pike of his own offense which was to be nothing more nor less than who he was. He had been in the wrong place at the right time.

And like him I too was nothing more nor less than who I was and what I was was a nothing, a nobody, with no power of nay-saying, pure and simple. Who was I to do anything to stop this mob? Who was I to cut down the burning priest who now was a conflagration of flames? And with that I sauntered off beyond the ring of fire into the ring of the dark forest and I ran through the dark forest that in truth wasn't forest at all but merely the county forest preserves. And I ran through it as if I had some-where I desperately needed to be even though there was nowhere else in this whole godforsaken world I could be because the world had rebuked me and it had rebuked me for being nothing more nor less than exactly who I was.

And I realized with the priest's death that I would fall like the common skunk falls because I was nothing more than a common skunk. I would lie dead where I fall only to be discovered as a flint of white bone poking out of the high grass some season hence by Blind-eyed Bob and his Second, Burp.

Fall dead. Unmoored. Unmourned. A skunk.

Part 4
The Hovel

Things sleep and when they are done sleeping they awaken and when they awaken we are either lucky or not so lucky to encounter them but it is in so encountering of them that we realize they are no longer sleeping but awake and ready to perform for us whatever it is they were designed to do when we had forgotten them in their sleeping place only to wait for that moment when we would encounter them and thus bring them back from their sleeping place to be for us what we had hoped they might be for us. And so it was with my hovel discovering it after that second time of escaping her place like a thief in the night only this time I left her place at high noon when she discarded me as the meaningless trophy I was no doubt soon to become discarded me to go off into the world and get her teeth fixed, perhaps. Or perhaps she had gone off into the world to do something else. I don't know. But I did know that this house was not the house for me and so I made good once again my promise to myself to escape this house and off I left like a thief in the night even though in point of fact it wasn't night but high noon when stepping out her door I crossed a road and then a berm and off I was once again strayed and lost in the woods looking for a hovel and from there hoping once again to make my way somehow or another back into the rebuking world that had rebuked me for reasons I still did not understand.

As I came into the woods I said to myself: I am back in the woods now back where I belong even though I knew that this was a lie. I spoke it anyway I had no other choice. If you entered into this woods a second time or even a third because the rebuking world couldn't contain you then you returned and said what was necessary whether it was a lie or no because to do any other thing than say what was absolutely necessary to do or say whether in fact it was true or not was the only way I discovered how to continue to deal with both the rebuking world and the shitty woods that I had been discharged into against my will even though this time it was my will to escape her house that had brought me here.

At the time she came for me I didn't know I belonged in the woods. At the time I met her I dreamt of nothing more than escaping these woods and that day she showed up to claim me seemed like the day my prayers had been answered—or if not my prayers for I didn't believe in the power of prayer although out in the woods there was always someone or another trying to convince you of the efficacy of prayer, that you could escape these woods through the *efficacy* of prayer but if by praying you could somehow through its efficacy escape these woods, then why were all of these stranded comrades who spent all day praying to leave these woods still stranded? And that's something my great mentor, Mike, would have asked: if prayer works, then what the hell are they still doing here? In any event I had been hoping and hoping to get out of these forest preserves but the problem is once you commit yourself to the forest preserves and you commit yourself to the forest preserves only on the day you decide to build your hovel in the deep woods far from where any person might be able to find you but once you commit yourself to the forest preserves then the whole problem of getting out of the forest preserves becomes the sole problem that slowly and inexorably takes hold of your life. Getting out of the forest preserves becomes such a mind-seizing problem that the only thing you can think about once you have committed yourself to the forest preserves is how in the world you're ever going to escape them. Oh sure, it may seem easy enough if you haven't committed yourself to the forest preserves to see a way out of the forest preserves in fact all sorts of people from town ambled through the woods that was adjacent to their community. They'd come out for an hour or two with the dog or on horseback and they'd use the forest preserve trails to come and observe a little bit of nature. The forest preserves were filled with nature: there were the great oaks and elms and some maple and pine and all the scrub brush and briars that blocked off large tracts of the preserve to casual tourists. But if you were one of these folks out visiting the forest preserves for a sunny afternoon walk in the woods then conceiving how to get out of the woods was the easiest thing imaginable. Why one only had to retrace one's steps to find the way back home. There were other sorts of visitors occasionally you might see people pitch a tent and spend the night camping which in these county forest preserves was actually illegal. I discovered it was illegal when I spied one morning a county forest preserve ranger writing up a husband and wife and two kids who had pitched a tent near their car and spent the early morning hour gathered around a small campfire frying bacon on a griddle and making s'mores for breakfast. But if you were one of these types then the way out of the forest preserves was also not only a solvable problem but also it didn't even present itself as a problem in the first place. If a problem fails to present itself then one has a hard time conceiving how there should ever be a problem at all and so leaving the woods was as easy as arriving and no sooner did these families leave the forest pre-serves behind them than they forgot all about them. They forgot as they went about their daily business that the woods continue

115

to exist on the periphery of their town, and while they went about their business, they forgot that the things in the woods went on about their business as well. They forgot because they had their business to attend to and all their errands to perform and the engagements of their interconnected social worlds that they plugged into and that took them away from this place, while we, stranded in these woods lacked exactly that: the means and the people and the wherewithal to plug back into the world out there and go about a normal sort of daily business. And while the visitors who came and left the forest preserves had no problem forgetting the forest preserves once they had left, those whom they left behind, those handful like me who had committed ourselves to the forest preserves never quite forgot about them. We spent our idle hours consumed with the thought of how easily they had come and gone. We would marvel at how they had come, spent a bit of time in recognition of the natural beauty and simple peacefulness the place had to offer, and then they went, forgetting just as soon as they left, that the woods ever existed. How wonderful it seemed to us who were stuck in the woods that they had even considered visiting these woods in the first place, and how wonderful still that they were so easily able to escape this place which—if you had committed to this place as we had committed to this place with our hovels nestled deep in the woods—was the most brutally difficult place in all of the world to escape. Once you had committed yourself to the woods, and these woods in particular, a force greater than gravity seemed to keep you here. Though it was easy enough to come into the woods and though it was easy enough to leave the woods, to those of us who had committed ourselves to the woods an invisible barrier seemed to rise up between us and the world

116

outside. Once you had committed yourself to the woods by building a hovel in the woods then the process of extricating yourself from the woods and figuring out how to reenter the world from which you had extricated yourself, prior to building your hovel, became such an intractable problem that those of us who were so marooned never left the woods. Sure there were those of us marooned here who died here and in a sense they escaped. But if you didn't want to die in these woods then the only option left to you was either to devise a means of escape back into the world or to persist indefinitely in your hovel in the woods. Since the former option of escaping these woods was virtually an insurmountable problem then the second option of persisting indefinitely became your plight. Once persisting indefinitely in these forest preserves became your plight then there were only two ways of accommodating yourself to your situation: you could either, as I had, learn to love at the level of instinct these woods in which you found yourself; the other way you could accommodate yourself to these woods was by allowing yourself to become consumed with the extraordinary problem of escaping these woods. If you ever met one of us stranded in these woods chances are you met a person who dreamt of nothing more fervently in all the world than escaping these woods, in fact the wish to escape these woods became such a fervent wish that the wish itself had incarnated itself as a primary feature of our various identities. Who am I? you might ask, if you were so inclined to ask, and though I am a man I might very reasonably and with great accuracy say: I am a fervent wish to escape these woods. I am the wish to leave these woods made incarnate in the form of a man who otherwise had committed himself to these woods by dropping anchor in the form of a hovel

117

deep in the interior of these woods. Though I too was not immune to the desire to escape these woods, I also knew it was a question of warding off madness not to submit to the desire to escape these woods. For once you gave yourself over to the desire to escape these woods the wish to escape achieved such a powerful hold over you that before long it became an obsession that drove you to madness. Once you heard one or another of us confess that we could think of nothing else in all the world than escaping these woods; once you heard one of us make this statement then you knew that the person uttering the phrase, though reasonably uttered in calm reassuring tones, was nevertheless so lost in a maze of obsessive madness that the madness itself became the thing one needed to escape. In other words the obsession to leave these woods became in itself an inescapable obsession from which one could only long to escape. How are you today, you might ask one of our fellow inmates and the fellow inmate might answer: I am an obsession to escape these woods, but the inmate might also just as well say—I am an obsession to escape the obsession that has seized me so completely that all I can speak of is this obsession. I am so thoroughly an obsession to escape these woods that should you ask me what the weather is or what time it is or hello how do you do, I only and always have only one response to you: I want to do nothing more than escape these woods. In other words the obsession to escape these woods became such an all-consuming obsession that the obsession itself seemed to erode the language of the obsessor down to simple phrases like this: I can't wait to get the hell out of this hell hole. Or, there is nothing more I desire than to get the hell out of this shit mire. Of course they might get so lost in their locutions of escape that I even heard it said once or twice: there is nothing

118

more I desire than to get the hell out of this shit's shire. As if the woods themselves were a shire of shit! But once one gave oneself over to the desire of escaping the woods—this shit's shire—then one threw up all hope of ever escaping these woods for the desire to leave these woods became such an obsession that the ability to solve the problem of escaping these woods became over-whelmed by the desire to simply leave them and so the calm careful meticulous planning that needed to be put in place to escape these woods was clouded over by the obsessing to do so and in effect one became rendered unable to escape these woods and what one became then was an inmate stuck in these woods who couldn't escape the wish to escape these woods and who writhed, as a result, with this fatal addiction to escape in the hovel or who stood outside the hovel and as happened from time to time the desire to leave and inability to do so incarnated itself as a howl and the howls you heard from the men who dreamt of nothing more than escaping this place were the most plaintive, strange, and haunting howls I have ever heard and whereas the howls of a wolf howling from the ridge were signals to all the wolves in the valley below, the howls of these men were nothing more than the simple howls of men who were beating their fists on the invisible barriers that had barred their escape from the one place that they desired above all else to escape: these woods that were in effect just the local county forest preserves to which we had for one reason or another inexplicably been banished.

And so that day she had come for me was a day that though I couldn't wish for it or long for it to happen, I nevertheless had to know or at least to intuit it deep in my being without acknowledg-ing that such an intuition lurked there. I had to know that some-thing or someone was coming sooner or later to rescue me else there is no way I would have been able to survive as long as I did some twenty-seven months in those forest preserves. If I wasn't going to desire above all else to escape these woods then I had to learn to love these woods on the level of instinct but in order for me to learn to love these woods on the level of instinct some deeper instinct that someone sooner or later was going to come and take me away from these woods had to announce itself to me in such a way that I didn't become like those others who sat all day watching the casual hiker wondering if he or she traipsing through the woods was going to be the one that had come to take them away from here. But that day she had come for me was a day like any other day. I had spent the morning lingering in my hovel which was barely large enough to accommodate my prone body. If I sat in my hovel cross-legged and straightened my back my head scraped the top of my hovel. It was a cocoon, really, not a home, not a tent. It was a place, worm-like, I lived in for twenty-seven months and I was prepared to continue to live in my hovel as long as necessary no time limit specified—for if I had thought I might get out at a specific time then my ability to per-sist relatively peacefully in these woods would be severely com-promised. So. I built my hovel and I built it myself from materials I had discovered in the woods or that I had scrounged from the roadside ditches that edged the perimeter of the woods. In this way I came to find large sheets or flanges of metal that had flown off the backs of trucks and tilted windside in the ditch, I recov-ered these flanges of metal and I found plywood and hauled it to my site and along the river I found pieces of timber from build-ings that had collapsed in the spring floods and I brought them to my site and I found a mattress washed up from the floods as well which I spent a week at the hand pump in the park washing

120

and drying and rewashing to clean the mud that had soaked into it. From these found elements and logs and timber and blankets that I had found that lovers would occasionally leave behind after fornicating in the meadow, I made my hovel. And then she came and took me away and after a while I had become a rumphulus whose sole purpose was to announce to no one because I had been discarded by her that she had been on a journey, which was really just her spying on me. Then I was discarded by her to collect dust and rust as if I were not a man but a tchotchke so that I knew as soon as I had a chance I would need to escape back into the woods, escape her place like a thief in the night though it was high noon. I left . . . I left the moment she decided to get her teeth fixed. I left and escaped back into the woods.

• • • •

What's it doing there, I thought to myself. Of all the places to put my hovel why did I build it there? For really even though the woods was a surprisingly well-defined and limited wilderness yet there were seemingly infinite places within these woods where one might build one's hovel and yet of all the places I could have built my hovel I chose this place only a hundred yards or so from the road to build mine. Only a hundred yards or so away from her wretched house where she, from her window, can observe me: my strengths (my ability to persist alone out here in this wilderness) and my weaknesses (my ability to persist alone out here in this wilderness). Standing on the edge of the road staring deep into the thicket of the woods I saw upon closer scrutiny my own hovel. What are you doing here? I asked out loud. It was my hovel whom I addressed of course and I didn't expect a reply yet during all those many months I lived in the forest preserves my own hovel became not merely a friend but an unspeaking intimate who listened intently to everything I happened to tell it. If it was raining for instance and I sought shelter from the storm within my hovel then I would speak tenderly to my little building telling it to hang in there and I often expressed my gratitude to it that it was able to stand up to the worst the weather had to give. Once in a hailstorm for instance it was pelted for several hours on end and I lay within its warm comfortable space grateful that it was able to withstand the brunt of the storm. The interior of my hovel was decorated with minute scratchings I made on the surface of the wall. Initially, I scratched the surface of the walls to indicate how many days had transpired since the world had rebuked me and sent me into this wilderness but with time other compulsions drove me to mark the walls. For instance, I would mark the wall whenever I encountered someone during the day. So if I ran into the priest or Adam or Hunter, for instance, I would make a little mark indicating I had made contact with one of the other stranded. I had another area on the wall of my hovel reserved for the markings that I had recorded of my meetings with Mike hand up, hi hi, tug at the beard and a look over the shoulder indicating whether I should follow or not. Were I to follow then I left one kind of hash mark; were I not to follow then I left a different kind of hash mark. Other times if I didn't see a person the whole day I would record the absence of running into anyone for the day, and then instead I would leave a marking to indicate I had seen a significant animal. If for instance I happened upon a large coon who was crawling out of a hole in the trunk of a nearby oak, I would indicate this sighting of a big coon by marking the wall of my hovel. It was in this way that my hovel became marked with hash marks and crosshatches that were really the personal diary of my very own experience in the woods that I had been rebuked into for reasons that I was never able to understand, and then I discovered that in addition to all of these markings that I liked the pattern the hash marks made on the inside of my hovel so I would produce more of them to increase and improve the design of my hovel and those markings, of which there were many, didn't record anything at all and so they were meaningless as so much of my time and my life, for that matter, was stranded in the woods all alone no way out. I was a nothing and a nobody and these miscellaneous designs which were of interest only to me confirmed that fact.

● ● ● ●

And there it was. Standing there all alone in the woods—my hovel—can you imagine the rain because it was spring? And the river had flooded a large expanse of the forest preserves and Mike was so long gone I was starting to forget who he was or why he was. I couldn't remember what the meaning of his life was much less could I remember the sound of his voice though I never forgot the beard and so to memorialize him I grew a beard of my own. I assumed he had become in his second life a skunk but a very particular type of skunk: he was the type of skunk who had figured out how to leave the woods and visit all the well-kept lawns of the houses in town. He had figured out how to raid their garbage cans for food and how to return as he pleased to the woods only to leave nocturnally the woods as he pleased for the town and then back again all by moonlight and craft and wit. He had learned, unlike the rest of us, how to come and go as he pleased.

123

He had learned to live as a common skunk without dignity but with the autonomy that dignity precludes to come and go under cover of night.

It was raining. Can you imagine the storm because it was spring?

I was lost in the spring storm overcome by rain when I stumbled upon my hovel. It was a makeshift hovel with a tenuous resistance to gravity: it would sooner or later collapse or be blown to smithereens by winds by storms and by the ruins of time . . . obliterated, gone. A memory and then not a memory. One day I would confess to myself how in the world I ended up here. One day I would confess all this to myself. But not right now. Today in the rain while my hovel is groaning in the storm, I will climb an old sycamore that I call Bill. I will climb the sycamore, my face lashed and whipped by the rain, and I will climb it as if it is the topmast of a galleon ship on the high seas even though it is only a modestly grown sycamore in the county forest preserves and in the high wind and rain I will climb that sycamore called Bill to its topmost branch and I will command the storm to blow and strike me down. Come on, I scream, strike me down! Strike me down in the high wind! Strike me down!

And I scream strange sounds in the high wind atop Syca-more Bill and I tug on my beard and I look over my shoulder and I scream for all I am worth trying to relieve myself of the pain . . . the unbearable pain of existence.

Coda

Where's the end of the world? I sometimes think that this place here, my shanty deep in the forest preserves, is the end of the world: the river flows by, the planes pass overhead, traffic shakes the trees around me—even so this is it—the end. I used to think that the end of the world was a place you arrived at as if it were some kind of destination as if you had to float down a raft to get there or take an airplane and like an arctic explorer have them air-drop you there. I think a lot of people try to find the end of the world just this way: is it the moon? is it the limit of the galaxy? is it the top of that mountain? In fact the end of the world is the exact opposite of these places and getting there requires the worst of all luck it's a place you arrive at precisely because you have no destination and when you get there you're surprised—shocked that not only have you finally arrived there but that you don't have any way out: radio contact with the world has failed. All bridges have been destroyed. It's been raining for six days and it takes all my effort to keep my camp in order—to keep dry. Welcome to the end.